MEET ME AT THE
RAINBOW BRIDGE

Also by Cheryl Price Morgan

Inspirational Self Help

A Journey Unfolding:

The Mystery of Trusting God

MEET ME AT THE
RAINBOW BRIDGE

LOVE IS NEVER LOST

CHERYL PRICE MORGAN

Dedication

I dedicate this book to my great-nieces Reese Noelle Brown and Sydney Elise Brown; to my own pets and visiting wildlife who've passed away; to animal lovers all over the world; and to Carina Chock who is sharing her creative artwork at a much younger age than I was able to begin sharing my gift of writing.

Contents

Acknowledgments   ix

Introduction   xi

Chapter 1   1
The Gates of Heaven

Chapter 2   9
Admission to Eternity

Chapter 3   17
Pet Angels

Chapter 4   25
A Gathering Place

Chapter 5   35
Timeless Waiting

Chapter 6   43
Sharing Stories

Chapter 7   51
Playful Pause

Chapter 8   61
Bridge in the Distance

Chapter 9   73
The Tunnel

Chapter 10   83
The Wild

Chapter 11   93
Birds of a Feather

Chapter 12   105
Coming Together

Chapter 13   119
Preparations

Chapter 14   129
Silk Threads

Chapter 15   141
The Crossing

Epilogue   153

Contact Cheryl Price Morgan   155

About the Author   157

Acknowledgments

I am grateful for all those in my life who kept me on the path leading to eternal life, and felt comfortable telling me the truth about when they thought I was making a mistake. No one is perfect, but if we look out for one another, we can catch a glimpse while on earth of what the promise of eternal life holds for us. It is beyond measure.

Special Acknowledgement to Carina Chock, who I commissioned to create the images for this book. She is a very promising and creative young artist with a great future ahead of her. I was able to write while looking at her sketches, and each image helped the words and stories flow.

Thank you, Carina!

Introduction

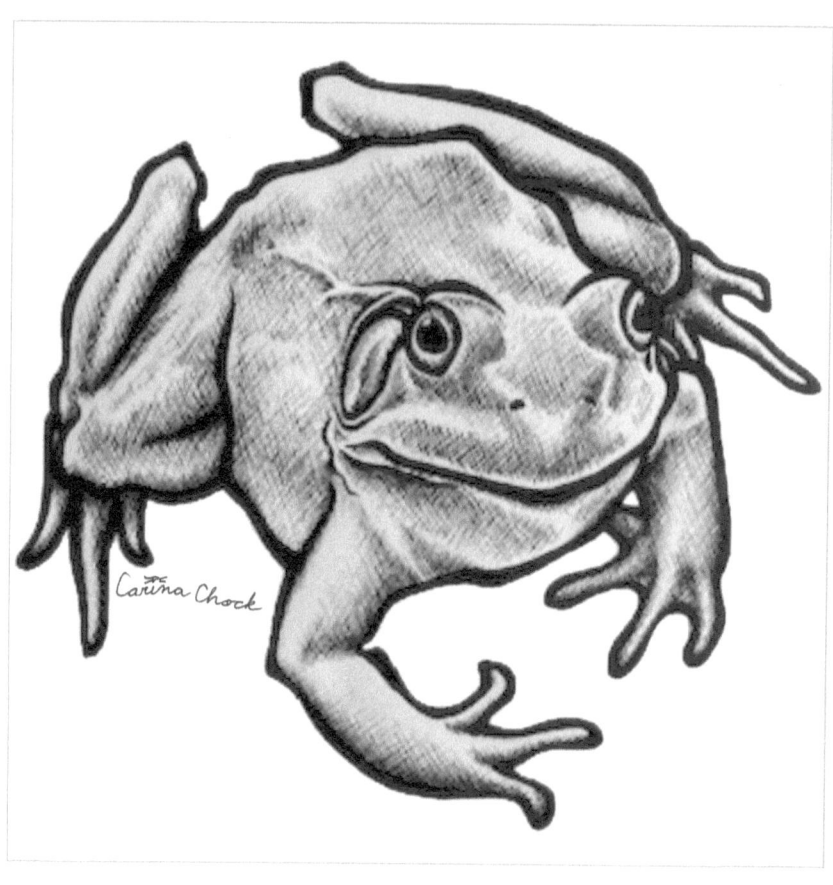

Animals are an important part of both nature and our lives. Though we can live closely with domesticated animals who can lovingly be trained, the behavior of wild animals needs to be understood and respected in order to live safely side by side. All living beings including animals have souls and a definite purpose in this life. One can speculate what becomes of them once they die, especially for the ones we've dearly loved. Is there any possibility we will see them once again? Imagining that makes our loss bearable.

We can observe animals in the wild and become aware of their habits. We need not worry about possible threats they may pose, because they pass through many areas and only stay for a short time. Many, however, pose no threat and each of us can take steps to ensure the safety of their young. It's human nature to do what we want to do, but how often do we consider how our actions might harm other living things? For example, driving too fast or with distraction can put animals in harm's way. There seem to be more and more animals lying dead at the side of the road; this is especially painful when they are young and don't yet realize the damage vehicles can do. Do their mothers grieve like a human mother would?

Many people wonder about life forms on other planets; I wonder about how to best love the animals and people here around us, especially those pets close to our hearts. I think that how we care for animals is a reflection of who we are and what we value. Many people have pets as children—it's an excellent way to learn how to care for other living beings as we watch them thrive and grow into loving members of our families. Our pets love and trust us. They also watch over us in kind and often can sense when we are ill or in danger before it becomes noticeable.

This bond of mutual love becomes very strong, and when the lifespan of our beloved pet comes to an end, a part of ourselves deep within also dies. We ask ourselves why it hurts so much. We ask whether or not we can ever recover. The answer is yes. At some point we remember them fondly and cherish the times we had together. Sometimes we ease the pain by getting another pet to love, which helps to fill the void; sometimes another pet finds us almost as if our lives are eternally intertwined without our awareness. Life goes on and we become ready to love again if we are willing to risk opening our hearts.

What about the wildlife that watches us and sometimes decides that we aren't a threat? They are a gift of friendship which asks for nothing from us. Trusting that we will not harm them, they give birth to their young around our homes. This can be a rabbit who digs a hole in our lawns to ready for birth or a robin who chooses to nest under our eaves, no matter how inconvenient. It could be a toad who jumps into places from which he cannot free himself. There are many animals around us who keep themselves hidden, yet we can find them if they trust us enough to reveal their presence to us.

This is all part of the circle of life, which is precious. There is a peace within nature just as there is beauty if we open ourselves up to it. Animals have much to teach us if we can begin to let go of the demands of life for a little while so we can look around us. If we look very closely, we will discover many things we never saw before. They have always been there but we never thought to look for them. They weren't our chief focus, but once we begin to look all around our environment, we find so much which truly defines life in its simplicity.

So let us begin to think of the pets we've lost so we can wonder what's become of their souls. Are they okay? Do they remember us? Do they still love us? Are they happy and healthy? We long to see them once again, but we don't know if we ever will. By extension, what will become of us when we die? It's an unknown we don't like to think about. Those we love who've passed away have never come back to tell us about what they've experienced. It's an unknown, and we feel more comfortable with certainty.

There's a poem that has been around for a number of decades that was thought to be anonymous. It's entitled "Rainbow Bridge," and it's been recently attributed to an eighty-two-year-old Scottish artist and animal lover by the name of Edna Clyne-Rekhy. She wrote it in 1959, when she was young. She describes a scene of pets waiting for their human owners; once the owners also die, the pets run to their owners and they greet each other. Then they walk across the Rainbow Bridge together, never to be separated again. She wrote the poem to ease her pain after losing her pet.

This poem touched me so very deeply after the loss of one our beagles. The veterinarian who cared for our pet through her death not only sent us a sympathy card with the poem, but also stamped our beloved Lady's paw print on the card for us to remember her by. So the scene this poem creates is near and dear to my heart. I do not mention the poem in this book because it is available in many forms on the internet, but I'm using it as a backdrop for what I think happens at this point in time from the pet's perspective.

Perhaps the loss of a pet would be easier if they could talk to us and comfort us. Perhaps if we could tell them how much we love them and miss them it would be tolerable, if we knew they understood what we are saying. But we can only imagine what they would think we've said, just as we can only guess what they're trying to tell us. Yet in this life on earth, there are many forms of language and expression; we can sometimes understand by mannerisms or gestures what is being said, but it doesn't feel enough.

Animals accept death far more easily than humans do. Maybe that's because they are more connected with the natural world than we are? The modern world moves us further and further away from nature as life becomes filled with more and more electronics and technology. This keeps us busy with all of the various paths technology takes us through, until the rabbit holes become deeper and deeper, sometimes leading nowhere. Sometimes the pace of life makes us realize that we need to get off the roller coaster of life for a while and rethink where we are headed.

Our pets keep us grounded. If we pay attention to their behavior while outside, we begin to wonder what they see and smell, or why they are paying attention to certain things we didn't even notice. It the same thing with wildlife that reveals itself in our surroundings. Do they feel comfortable with us? Do they trust us? Why do they remain instead of moving on? What do they want from us, and how do they know for certain that we won't hurt them? Why do birds choose to nest near us? These are things to ponder as we look around at the natural beauty we see when we have time to look. This helps us to reconnect with the natural order of which we are a part but have forgotten.

So then let's delve into the potential within the minds of our pets and wildlife. It could be another exciting world of which we are unaware. Our focus can become very narrow as we deal with the details of modern life, however, as we open our minds to new things, we become acclimated to occasionally shifting the paradigm of reality to look at how other beings view their world. So I invite you to enter the world of animal-speak within the pages of this book. It holds much promise in conveying the inner world of the pets and wildlife we love and with whom we have connected. They love us as much as we love them, and they are waiting until the appointed time of our return to them.

Let us begin with introducing our narrator, the old American toad, who I rescued from a recessed basement window well along with his family many times. I saw him on the lawn one evening and said "hello" to him—it was as if he was waiting for me. He didn't move, and I told him that he needed to tell his family that it's dangerous to fall into the window well, that if I don't notice they're there, they will die from the hot sun in the summer months. Of course, he didn't reply, but he kept watching me. Then I also told him that he needed to go into the trees, because I didn't want my dogs to see him.

Then later, one night when I took my dogs out for their last walk, I saw the old toad on the driveway near the lamp post. It was a rather chilly night, and I told him that he needed to find some cover to stay warm. My dogs did go up to him to sniff and touch their noses to him, but they didn't try to harm him in any way. So we all said our good nights.

I went outside the next morning to get the newspaper, and I noticed that the old toad was still in the driveway. It was unusual that he would've remained there, and I grew sad to think that he had passed away that night. I touched him and confirmed that he had indeed died. I was moved to emotion to think that the old frog took the time to see me to say goodbye. Animals don't speak to us, but their actions communicate with us if we are open to watching them.

This old toad made an effort to establish a relationship with me, and for that I'm very grateful. I learned much from him about occupying this planet and how we are all capable of living peaceably together if we so choose. He showed me the wonder of nature, which we don't need technology to cherish. His impact on my very being is why I made him the narrator of this book. I hope that you can find some commonality with animals and with each other as you see life, love, and grief of the animals we've lost, through the perspective of an old American toad.

Chapter One

THE GATES OF HEAVEN

W hoa!! Where am I?

I remember that I was on the ground near the woods, but it was getting so cold! I stayed near the woman, the one who had rescued me from a window well when I couldn't jump out. It was her dog who alerted her that I was in the window well, and she started keeping watch every day after that. She checked on me and my family daily to see if we had become confined so we couldn't eat or find water.

This last time she saw me was in the driveway after dark when she took her dogs out. I felt a nose nudge me, but the dog didn't hurt me. He was just curious, I guess. They went in for the night, but I had no way of telling the woman that I wasn't feeling well. I'm an old toad and I knew my time of death was near. I moved closer to the edge of the lawn by the driveway and tried to find some area of warmth, but more importantly I wanted to be where she would find my body in the morning.

I saw the woman approach my body cautiously. Both she and her dog nudged me, but I didn't respond. She instinctively knew that I had died, but perhaps she thought that I went into hibernation for the night and that I would revive once the cold air had warmed. I saw that she came out to check on me—I was no longer in my body—and she realized that my body was lifeless. She shook her head and frowned. I was not surprised at her sadness, as I'd been around for a couple of years, and she had been kind to me.

She picked my body up to bury it rather than just toss it into the woods where an animal could eat it. It does matter when we care about other living beings, although we may not see the effect of our caring for years to come. We are all connected in some way, even if there are no words between us. I knew by this woman's actions that I was safe. I had seen her with her dogs and with other living things—she watched out for all of us. She understood the meaning of life and soul-full living. Time isn't just for now, but rather that this present moment shines for all eternity.

I left wherever I was when I had a body, and it remains a distant memory. This new place is unknown but not frightening, there is a certain peacefulness around it, but I am floating through clouds upon clouds that I can't see through. I'm not sure how much time has passed, nor do I know how I'm traveling without a body. I'm very aware of my consciousness though, and I perceive everything in my surroundings. Where am I? Will I reach a destination at some point? What will happen to me? This is all unknown, but I seem to be taking a trip.

Yes, that's it! I'm taking a trip with an unknown destination.

I'm no longer sure of when I left my body, but I'm beginning to sense something way off in the distance. This is difficult for an old toad like me, and I no longer have eyes or ears or nostrils to discover where I am. The sense I am now using is something totally different from anything I've ever experienced. I think it may be the essence of who I am, which is purer than when I was in my body; I sense it is my soul and that I'm part of God's creation, but what is my purpose? I hope this journey will answer my questions.

I can see something! It's as if I am being pulled toward it, because I didn't set out to find it. Am I in a tunnel? Maybe, but it isn't dark; rather it is full of light. The light is a beacon showing me where and how to move. It is leading me and I feel complete trust. As I move further along my path, I begin to see a structure coming into view. It is very inviting and I feel drawn toward it by the power of love. It's not a momentary feeling that passes in a fleeting manner, but rather it feels like the everlasting experience of eternal love. I know I'm loved, because I still have my consciousness, or my essence; this love is embracing me like a soft cocoon.

I have no idea how long I've been traveling, but I'm beginning to see a structure, which looks like a closed gate surrounded by clouds. Yes, it is a gate—it's very clear now, and I can see a lion and lamb in front of it. I don't feel afraid. They were adversaries on earth. Could they now be companions? They are peaceful together and they look as if they are waiting, but I don't know for whom—it can't just be for me. They look young and seem to complement one another. The lion represents the dangers in the world known as Earth, while the lamb represents the possibility of the gentleness of mankind in eternity. Yet here they are subdued, or perhaps just filled with peace.

I'm very close to them now, yet I am not afraid of what is to come. I feel welcome, as if I'm exactly where I'm supposed to be.

I ask the lion, "Where am I?"

He replies, "You are at the Gates of Heaven."

I look at the lamb and ask, "How do I gain entry?"

The lamb says, "If you have arrived here, you are already guaranteed admittance. However, the gates will not open until the appointed time, so please wait patiently."

I ask both of them how long they have been waiting. Both say they will remain here until all those meant to be in Heaven arrive. I mention that it must feel like a long time, to which they both reply that there is no awareness of time here. I thank them and begin to focus on who "I AM."

My awareness begins to increase in acuity. My perception of my surroundings becomes more fluid as I adjust to being outside my toad body. The clouds I have been immersed in move around and thin out. I can see other animal souls moving about, and I adjust to how communication transforms from words to thoughts, which every being seems to understand. I reach out to them but end up going through them. They are as aware of me as I am of them, we connect and communicate without form, but I don't yet understand how this is happening and what will come next. Who and what are we waiting for? Where are the people and birds and fish I know were with me on earth? I miss them.

I begin to focus on the Gates. I am in front of one, but there are many. Everyone seems to know which Gate they are to be at until the appointed time. We are not alone—even an old toad can sense that. How do I hear without ears, or see without eyes? Or do I still have them somewhere? This is so difficult to understand. The Gates are mesmerizing and I perceive that my Gate is pulling me near. I'm watching and listening for clues about what is to happen next. Then suddenly there are doves hovering around the Gate, their wings are musical and soothing. I keep watching them as do those around me. Then the sound of the wings begins to direct the doors of the Gates to move. Our souls yearn in unison and we begin to understand that the path to eternal life is beautifully orchestrated with love. Life never ends; there are only new beginnings.

Chapter Two

ADMISSION TO ETERNITY

The Gates begin to open in unison ever so slowly. The doves flying above are directing their movement. They are so big and far reaching to an old toad, but it appears that everyone's soul is similar in size. I keep watching the doves. Their movements look purposeful, although I don't understand how they know what to do in order to convince the doors to move. How can inanimate objects sense music and respond to it? How can Gates without eyes or ears respond to the rhythm of the doves' wings flapping? Yet they do.

Finally, the doors stop moving, staying halfway open. Thick clouds move toward the opening, and it's impossible to see through them, but the lion and the lamb have directed us to wait until we are called. We continue to watch the doves—they are increasing in number but their wings are no longer making any sound. The souls of everyone waiting move in closer together. We comfort each other because everyone has left loved ones behind. The doves also draw closer to each other. There is a purpose for this, although what our souls experience isn't immediately clear. The closer the doves gather, the greater the peace we all feel.

We take in this peacefulness. The cooing of the doves is very soothing and we begin to sway in unison to no particular beat of music or sound. Our souls expand and start to pulse with the connection we feel with each other, and we enjoy this sense of communion. The more we begin to connect, the sweeter the cooing of the doves becomes. There are no differences now, there is only a coming together and a homecoming.

At some point we all become aware that the doves have begun to speak to us. We listen intently as they prepare us for what comes next, and we all hear what is said in our own languages. We are told that our souls need not be afraid, for we have left pain and suffering behind. We will experience the joy of living in the world prepared us for, and we only have to take in the fruits of our labor. Our souls will expand as we fill with eternal joy, and peace is the stimulus facilitating the expansion into eternal life. However, this expansion is not in size but rather in the fullness of our souls. It will happen naturally, so we just have to trust that eternal life is a new realm of existence. The doves continue to explain that it's not really new, we have just forgotten from whence we came.

The doves continue to tell us that we will slowly begin to remember, but entering eternal life is very much a transition from the earthly bodies that encased our souls. We were restricted while within our bodies, and perhaps that's why so many desire freedom—yet true freedom isn't experienced until our souls leave our bodies, because it's within those earthly vessels where we experience aging, pain, loss, and suffering. There are positive experiences too, but life on earth is always mixed with joy and sadness, pleasure and pain, love and hate, good and bad, and so on. Life in our bodies is a preparation of our souls for life eternal, if we pay attention to the details of what we are experiencing and how we deal with it.

As the doves continue, we listen closely and learn that we will begin to see those on earth we've loved and left behind. It is the bonds of our love that allow us to remain near our cherished ones even though we cannot be seen by them— sometimes those who are spiritually sensitive can sense a breakthrough of our souls through the veil separating heaven and earth, but it is only a very short visit. Still, it provides comfort to those we love knowing that they aren't alone, even if they feel that way. It also provides hope that they will see us again. It is this hope that sustains life on earth, and the effects are everlasting.

We don't feel the need to ask the doves any questions, because they anticipate every one of our thoughts and concerns. It was amazing how quickly we trust in their goodness, just as we feel the protection of the lion and the lamb. We want to know more of what is to come, yet our curiosity is tempered by the joy of what we are experiencing in the present moment. Maybe that's what God kept trying to tell us? Stay in the present moment because the past is gone and the future hasn't yet arrived; savor what we can experience from the present moment, and this will help us build the memories we need to sustain the future and understand the past.

This is quite a lot of thought for an old toad, especially because mankind thinks I am an inferior species. However, I experience quite a bit within the environment of my simple life. Some humans would agree that simplicity is better for the soul because this helps the soul stay focused. Simplicity and nature help us to connect with the world around us. Yet mankind has so many increasing demands upon its time, which pulls humans away from the very fiber of themselves and who they truly are—that is, unless every being keeps life and its happenings in perspective.

I see my life pass before me now. I am reviewing scenes just as I would while watching a movie if I were human. Yet the place where I find myself now doesn't separate souls by the bodies that encased them on earth—all are equal and valued by God. The skin color we had on earth is gone, the things we possessed on earth are no longer with us, genders do not matter here because there is no need for reproduction. Love is what binds us together and beckons us to the place where we now find ourselves. I know this now, but it's a realization that mostly comes with age. I'm not sure how I came upon what most would call *wisdom*. Maybe I grew into it, or perhaps it was always there waiting for me to find it.

I begin to notice the doves once again. They are flapping their wings with an increasing intensity and heightened crescendo. Ever-so-slowly the Gates of Heaven begin to move once again. The clouds thicken and become denser; they aren't dark and foreboding, but rather are a bright, fluffy white, reflective of the anticipation of what's on the other side. It's the great unknown, which unfolds as we begin to experience our souls expanding with the recollection of what we once were, before we were born into a body while living on earth.

My soul and the other waiting souls are prohibited from moving forward by the pressure the clouds create. It feels like a zero-gravity state where we are just floating. The end of the tunnel we came through pushes us forward and the clouds push us back in equal measure. We have no choice but to enjoy the peace of the moment. Time has stopped for us, and we must acclimate to the inertia holding us still, just as our bodily forms held us encased in a structure given to us at birth.

Again I think back to when I was inside a physical body. There were many small, young toads I taught to survive. Many got caught in places they couldn't climb out of, but in the last place I inhabited the woman looked out for us. She watched carefully ever since her dog let her know we were there. This helped to reinforce what I was teaching. It's good to know that some souls carry the gift of compassion for other living creatures, because this means more within God's creation than most realize.

"What goes around, comes around" isn't just a saying. It means that whatever we give to or do for others has a way of coming back to us. If we do good, others who do good are attracted to us. If we do evil, evildoers are attracted to us. If we are cruel, we surround ourselves with cruel indifference. This is a choice all forms of life make, and then we live with either the fruits or consequences of those choices—it's each soul's decision to make.

Compassion feeds the soul when it is profoundly experienced during times of need. It imbeds itself in our very being and nourishes us just like food. Once we take in our fill and water it with gratitude, we can pass it on to others, who then pass it on to others: this begets a circle of love for those living things around us, human and otherwise. It makes the world a better place for those who are the beneficiaries of random acts of kindness, but it's also in the very act of giving that each receives accordingly.

Suddenly, I notice that the doves have stopped moving and cooing as they rest upon the top of the Gate. They are waiting at attention, drawing all of us waiting souls into silence. Nothing is happening. It's as if time is standing still. Then ever so slowly the gates begin to move inward as they open inviting us in. The white clouds begin to stir and swirl with purposeful activity that we cannot foresee. We wait in quiet anticipation. We gently move together as if our souls are being merged into one eternal communion of peace. The Gates have separated fully and the clouds begin to thin as they disperse. Finally, we are able to see the Light. We are home.

Chapter Three

PET ANGELS

Carina Chock

I see it! I'm looking at a glimpse into heaven as the clouds fully dissipate. Our waiting souls don't move. A beagle with angel wings approaches us as if floating in the air. He stops at the gate entrance and looks deep into all of our souls. He is pleased.

"You have made it," he says. "I've been waiting until all of the souls meant to be here now have arrived."

The beagle angel asks us to follow him into paradise. We cross through the Gate and wait for further instruction before continuing our journey. The beagle angel explains that there are many animals who have become angels in order to guide souls to the waiting place, and we are to wait there until our loved ones arrive. The place will sustain us until the appointed time when we reunite with our loved ones. We will be able to bask in the Light, enjoy each other's company, and play to our heart's content.

We are each assigned an animal angel to help us adjust to our new environment. The beagle explains, "The animals God has chosen to be angels are also still waiting for their loved ones. Each one given the wings of service has been granted the gift of understanding the needs of others in order to best serve particular souls. Each of you will be assigned an angel until you no longer need one to guide you. Then if an angel sees his loved one approaching in the distance, you will receive his wings as a gift to help another soul about to enter paradise."

I was amazed that this honor could be granted to a lowly old toad. I'm glad that I was able to find the woman who loved me. Now I have someone to wait for, so we can walk into eternal life together. Life on earth can be solely about survival in a toad body —actually, survival can be the primary focus in any body, human or otherwise, if we let it.

There is no status or rank in heaven, however, only individual souls. Each soul is the particulate essence of life, similar to one small cell within an organism. It's the combination of a number of small cells which allow the parts of the organism to function, and if all of the parts function well together, then the organism is able to survive. Each cell, or soul, has a particular function to learn and grow into. It's the nourishment of the cell or nurturing of the soul which allows life to successfully continue. Kindness matters, as does understanding, accepting differences, and seeing life through the eyes of those not like us, no matter what physical body they've been born into. This allows us to adapt and evolve as our environment changes.

I turn my attention again to the beagle angel. He looks at the group he has led through Heaven's Gate, and begins to slowly move his wings back and forth as he surrounds us with God's love. We all watch and become mesmerized at the calm this creates. The beagle angel knows exactly what he's doing, because we all begin to relax as we get used to existing outside of our bodies. It's amazing to observe the transparency of each other's soul as we begin to really see each other for who we are. We've yet to realize our purpose as very essential beings who are part of a perfect being, Our Creator. This is all a new experience.

The beagle angel points to a bridge in the distance. He calls it the Rainbow Bridge. Its colorful display interspersed with a cloudy mist holds our attention, as there's an energy there which acts like a magnet. Our souls are drawn toward its majestic beauty.

The beagle continues, "Once your loved ones arrive, you will walk across the Bridge hand in hand, never to be separated again. The love that you've experienced for a short while on earth will never end in Heaven. It will be rich and complete, because you won't be limited by earthly bodies. Your thoughts will be full of the life God wants you to have as you finally arrive home to the place that has been prepared for you."

I look around and see others moving around the grassy meadow reflecting some of what life on earth was for each of us. However, what each of us sees is different from every other soul. We all lived on earth, but it was in different realms where we needed to share the same space and get along. How can we all be different in the way we experience the same thing? How can we all think different thoughts when we interact with others, and why do those differences matter? All souls struggle to make sense of the space we find ourselves in, and in the midst of that struggle we try to accommodate the differences of others but often fail. Why wasn't I aware of this while I was in my body? Why did I need to leave my body in order to begin to see that it's in our differences that we move toward the whole? Once we begin to accept one another for who they actually are, we stop seeing others as a reflection of ourselves.

I am just beginning to see my soulful existence with a little more clarity but I'm still confused as to why I'm beginning to realize how much I actually don't know. Maybe that's the beginning of wisdom? Yet I've left earth and my body, so does it really matter that I am still learning?

I see the beagle angel studying me, so I ask, "I seem to be the same as I was on earth except that I have no physical form. I'm still thinking, asking myself questions, and processing what I'm experiencing, so where am I?"

The beagle angel smiles and replies, "You are in a place close to Heaven waiting for a loved one to join you. You remain your thoughts. What you thought about or paid attention to on earth remains with you in eternal life, so it's best that all souls focus on the positive or the good. While there is suffering on earth, it is a hard task master. Yet its purpose is to teach and allow all souls to grow and mature. If everyone is comfortable and never experiences hardship, there is no reason to change any part of your situation on earth. Everything becomes stagnant, and those who only know comfort think that everything will be given to them without any thought or effort on their part. Never having challenges doesn't make anyone resilient, because they never have to change. Suffering, if handled properly, forces growth because no one likes pain."

I think about this for a moment. I certainly don't like pain for myself or my family. The beagle angel is patient as I try to think about what question will make sense right now. He moves his wings slowly, and I feel the breeze of clarity refresh my soul.

I ask, "Does God cause suffering, or does He allow it? Why?"

The beagle angel looks over to the Rainbow Bridge and says, "You will have a full understanding once you enter eternal life. No, God doesn't cause suffering. He allows it because He gave free will to all souls born on earth. Their physical bodies allow them the opportunity to act on what they decide to do."

He continued, "Sometimes those on earth choose good either for themselves or others. Sometimes they choose evil out of misguided anger. At other times they simply make mistakes. Yet all of these actions, which are the result of what was first a thought, impact other souls in many ways, which weren't realized when the decision was made. Sometimes others get hurt as a result of someone else's decision; God didn't cause or allow that. Life on earth is imperfect because every living soul is imperfect. Yet without free will or the ability to choose, there can be no love. God loves us enough to let go of us for a while to be on our own. If we come back to Him, it's because of love that we've chosen to do so. If you force someone to return or do what you want, that's coercion rather than love given freely."

I look around the meadow and see all of the souls waiting for loves ones. They are free to walk across the Rainbow Bridge at any time if they don't want to wait. But then they will not know the joy of reuniting with those they've loved at the very moment they walk through Heaven's Gate. I will choose to wait, just as these other pet and wild animal souls are patiently waiting. I will mingle and learn about all of the different experiences every soul brings to this waiting place. I choose to enrich my thoughts to increase my fullness of life once I walk across the Rainbow Bridge into eternity. My wait begins.

Chapter Four

A GATHERING PLACE

I'm amazed at the beauty I see on this side of Heaven's Gate. There is green meadow as far as the eyes can see, with ponds and trees and plants galore. There are toys and shaded resting places....and way in the distance I can see the Rainbow Bridge.

It looks like the countryside on earth, and there's such an indescribable sense of peace and anticipation. The bridge goes over a river, but there is some force preventing us from approaching it. I can see the entrance to the bridge, and beyond that thick clouds obscure the view.

Many animals are here with me in this place, and it's amazing to the wide variety of those who have passed through the gate. We have an opportunity to watch, listen, and learn from all of the experiences of the various animals with whom we've been brought together.

I see dogs, cats, birds, deer, pigs, coyote, bears, and many other types of animals—all come together without any threat of harm or rejection. Each one feels comfortable with the others around them. We've left our bodies behind but our souls continue to think and perceive. It's utterly amazing and it's something I don't quite understand.

My mind races trying to figure out what is going on. I know I died, but I'm still alive through my consciousness. How can I be aware if I have no visible form? Why hasn't my thinking stopped just as my heart did? I perceive all of these different animals. I recognize them for what they are, even though they also have left their animal bodies, and they recognize me. I wonder what consciousness, communication, and thought really are. I don't understand how they can continue after death, but I do know that I'm experiencing the same things I did while on earth. I'm being repetitive as my thoughts race. What is this new place where I don't need food, water, or shelter? None of us do. We are just able to wait for whatever is to come next.

However, if there is no passing of time, is *waiting* the proper term to describe what all of us here are experiencing? When time is infinite, can we perceive it as passing? Perhaps it is more like our living in a constant state of being? We would never perceive this as being possible while in our bodies, because time always passes on earth—yet what we do experience on earth adds to the memories in our consciousness. So I haven't lost those memories and they are sustaining me now. This is all so new to me, but I'm learning that life on earth isn't the end, but rather the beginning of the continuation of life.

I am deep in thought when I become aware of the close presence of another soul. I am experiencing a connection with one of the animals here who I recognize as a German Shepherd. I say "connection" because we have no eyes or ears, or any other senses we used while in our bodies. Yet it's a strong perception that he is near as our thoughts pass back and forth between us. Yes, that does make it difficult to hide things we don't want others to know about us and our thoughts. The German Shepherd wants to tell me about his life on earth, and how it wasn't always easy; yet he was loved, and he loved his human in return. He still actively loves him and is sad that his human has grieved for him all of the time he's been gone. He watches over his human still, and he very much would like to tell him that he hasn't lost him. He so much wants to tell him that there will come a time when they will reunite.

The German Shepherd doesn't feel sadness about God calling him home to eternity. It was his time, his work on earth was finished. That doesn't make it easier for his human to find comfort and deal with his loss. He wishes that his human understood that death isn't permanent but rather a transition to a life that is infinite. Our souls live on in different outward appearing forms. That's why it's so important to not judge by appearances, whether it be human or animal. There is something more.

The German Shepherd goes on to share his story with me. He says, "I was abandoned as a puppy. I went through several foster homes but no one wanted to adopt me. I had much love to give someone, but I was deaf. My deafness made me untrainable, or so people thought. No one wanted to take a chance on me. Who wanted a watch dog who couldn't hear?"

I reflect on this and think about how unimportant that is in eternity where no one has ears to hear. I wait with anticipation to hear the rest of the German Shepherd's story; sometimes we all have to wait for the right person to come along.

"Then one day a boy saw me," the Shepherd continues, "and was captivated by the thought that no one wanted me. The young boy understood what that felt like because his mother had given him up for adoption. As a teenage girl who was unmarried, she couldn't care for him, so he was placed in foster care. The boy didn't find someone to adopt him until he was seven because he was also deaf." The German Shepherd pauses. "The boy was amazed that he had found a dog just like him. We became fast friends. We taught each other, but most of all we had the patience to give to each other the unconditional love we both needed."

I say, "That's so important. It's often difficult for people to just accept other living beings for who there are, with all of their weaknesses and faults. The earthly bodies we are given have genetic mistakes sometimes."

He agrees. We both ponder about our own imperfections, but we also speculate that perhaps they are meant to direct us on our individual journeys. Often times people try to socialize children and animals into what they think is appropriate development, without considering what the children and animals really need based upon who they are. Socialization is important for both society and the animal kingdom, but the gifts each soul brings to the earthly life need to be nourished and developed. No one can be truly happy by being forced to live their life as someone else sees them, rather than who they truly are.

The German Shepherd goes on to share what his life with the boy was like. He lovingly reminisces about the bond they shared as he speaks. "We took some time to just be with each other. That involved sharing toys, food, and running in the backyard. I wanted to please him and he wanted to love someone. Over time we developed hand signals because we both couldn't hear. The reward for connecting was kind touches and smiles. The boy spent much time teaching me commands and to do tricks, and I never got tired of responding. Time went by and we were the best of friends until it was time for him to go away to college."

Yes, time passes and creates restrictions we all need to manage. I enjoy listening to the many ways both the German Shepherd and the boy did things together for many years—the time forged an unbreakable bond which was everlasting. It was happiness and memories in the making for both of these souls. So many don't realize how these experiences sustain throughout life and beyond, but it's never too late to begin creating them. All it takes is looking away from the technology of our times and refocusing on the nature, people, and events surrounding us. There's much to see if we only stop what we're doing and appreciate the quietness of life.

The German Shepherd continues, "The boy grew into a fine young man who was thoughtful and caring. He wanted to help others just as we both had been helped by those around us. He studied hard in college as I grew old. We both knew my time on earth was coming to an end. I waited for him to come home between semesters. I wanted to experience his hugs one more time. The young man went to sleep one night, and I joined him on his bed just as I always had. I pressed my back into his legs as he fell asleep. I was now once again perfectly content. I rested in his love and took a deep breath. Then I exhaled my last."

I am deeply touched by what the German Shepherd was able to closely experience with a human. It's not something that old American Toads can do daily. We flourish in our own environment with our own toad family, and we keep watch. We observe what's going on around us and we note the kind people we encounter. That is enough for us, as our security is living in our natural habitat. We see and understand more than people think we do. We are small and some people don't think twice about hurting us. That is their loss, because our souls will continue to live once we have left our earthy bodies. I'm living proof as I convey this story.

The German Shepherd explains, "I still am able to see my fine young man who has been fully grown and with a family of his own for quite some time now. He is aging just as I did, and I am waiting for his time to leave his earthly life."

The German Shepherd has no doubts about seeing his beloved companion once again, although the time for his arrival into eternal life is unknown to all but God. It's amazing that God understands that some people don't believe in Him, but He is very patient with his Creation. His existence doesn't depend upon people recognizing Him, although all animals see Him. God just is. He waits for people to experience their lives and then leads them back to where their souls first came from.

As I listen to the German Shepherd, he begins to watch the Gate through which he came many years ago. His anticipation is growing as the souls of people trickle through. They enter the green meadows just as we did, but there is no recognition of any of us who've been waiting. Then all of a sudden it happens! The soul of the German Shepherd and the soul of the boy-turned-man are merged in a cloud of love, the mist of which brings them ever so close once again. I'm not sure how the German Shepherd knew his boy was coming, because I'm still waiting for the woman who helped me return to my eternal home.

They are happy as they enjoy the beautiful meadow and reflect upon all of the time they spent together. There are no words here. There's only the communication between those who've deeply loved and understand the language of their souls fully recognizing the other as they were created. I continue to watch as the wings of the beagle angel create a path of vibrating wind to push them gently toward the Rainbow Bridge. Once they are there and are given permission to cross, they see others they've loved who've gone before them. Now united in love after their long wait to see each other once again, they cross the bridge together and enter eternal life never to be separated again. Time doesn't exist in Heaven, only the continuous communion of souls surrounded by love.

Chapter Five

TIMELESS WAITING

The best way to describe how I move within the green meadow is *floating*. I seem to be like a cloud, because I don't seem to be doing anything to generate movement. I just pass through various scenes and take notice. Then once in a while I feel like I'm supposed to focus on another soul—it was this way with the rabbit soul I perceive before me. I concentrate on his presence as he does the same with me. A sense of familiarity begins to grow stronger, until I fully recognize why I know him. We both were cared for by the woman!

He moves closer to me and we relive our experiences with her. The rabbit reminisces as he says, "She screamed the first time she saw my siblings and me in our nest on the ground. She was frightened because she didn't know what we were. My smaller sibling was curled up in a ball sleeping, and I was looking straight at her. She quickly covered us back up! She started discussing us with her husband as both kept their dogs away from us. She said she needed to research what we were because we looked like snakes."

I took in what the rabbit said because I don't know what a "research" is. I am perplexed by these human terms, and I'm not even sure if they are meaningful to my life. Humans are confusing. They spend so much time dashing around, and talking to whoever is nearby. My family and friends just live in whatever situation our environment presents to us. We don't worry about it, but rather adjust to whatever works. We just live in the present. We innately know that we aren't guaranteed tomorrow and we're okay with that. It's the ebb and flow of life.

The rabbit laughingly continues with his story, "She did figure out that we were baby rabbits! She had never seen a newborn before, and she didn't realize that we are gray and hairless when first born."

I must say that I didn't know that either. Our babies are fully formed miniatures of us with the same color. This just proves that every species has its own intricate design and why we should appreciate the differences we see. It makes life on earth so interesting.

The rabbit appreciatively explains, "Once the woman understood us, she took great care to cover our nest back up and placed chairs over us to protect us from the lawn mower and other wild animals which might be interested in eating us. She was careful to leave enough space for our mother to get in to feed us. She doesn't know how much we appreciated her kindness, but I will tell her some day when I see her."

The rabbit continues, "The woman checked on us daily to make sure we were okay and were still in the nest. She now knew that when she sees a pile of brown grass with some rabbit fur on it she needs to look for baby rabbits, so we were her teachers. We stayed in our nest for two weeks. During this time, we grew in both brown fur and size. We were still small but we left the nest to explore our environment a couple of days before permanently leaving. She knew we were getting ready when she lifted the chairs and saw that one of us was missing, and our mother also fled to seek cover."

It's amazing how we learn about each other if we are open to new experiences without judging or acting out of fear. The woman didn't quite know what to make of toads in window wells, but she knew that we couldn't get out without help. She was very sad when she missed seeing a few of my kin and they died. That strengthened my connection with her as love and compassion form strong bonds. This shows us that bonds between others are often formed without words and conversation. Actions speak louder than words. What we experience by watching the behavior of others has a great impact. Compassion never ends when it positively impacts lives with goodness.

The rabbit continues conveying his experience with the woman, "She saw me return to the nest after I had finished exploring. Then it was my sibling's turn, but he was smaller than me and more fearful. She found him huddled against her house's foundation near the window well. He wasn't moving. He was shaking and curled in a ball. She picked up a small shovel and carefully scooped him into it. She was able to get him back to our nest even though he tried to jump off the shovel. When she got close enough, he scurried back to the nest as quickly as he could. This brought a smile to her face."

I actually saw the woman do this, and then I knew she could be trusted. I watched her care for the rabbits just as she cared for my family's baby toads. So one day I also took a jump into the window well, and I sat there waiting for her. I looked at her as she approached with the curved shovel to help me out. I didn't try to get away as she carefully laid the shovel in the window well. I willingly jumped onto it and she brought me closer to the trees for shade and moisture. I visited the woman periodically because I liked her kindness even toward as small a creature as me, and I'm large for an old American toad.

The rabbit begins to explain how he ended up in eternal life and the green pasture. He says with sadness, "She looked out for us when she walked her two dogs. She didn't want them to unintentionally hurt us. I was out of the nest as I prepared to say goodbye. It was time to hop away and start my own life. However, her rat terrier saw me before she did. Rat terriers are bred to hunt rodents, so he did his job. He pounced on my two-week old body, and I cried out in fear."

"That's when the women saw me in the tall grass. She tried to pull back her dog's leash, but she wasn't quick enough. He pounced again and landed on my chest. The woman distanced the dog and came over to me with such a sad look. I look up and gazed into her eyes with the same love as when she first saw me and screamed. This time though she had tears in her eyes as I closed mine and died right in front of her. She took her dog inside and buried me along the trees near her windows where she often looks out. I will never forget her and the bond of love we shared."

I watched her bury the baby rabbit even though she didn't know that I was there. She did what was right by such a small creature, even though some would consider this inconceivable to care so much about something so insignificant. The woman knew that no life form created by God was insignificant, and so do I. It all matters. None of us ever knows when we're being watched by another human or animal, or even by God. Someday we'll all be surprised by the account presented to us as we try to respond to the memories.

The rabbit looks at me and says it is time for him to play in the green pasture. It will be a while before the woman passes through the gates, but he says he will look for me when she does. We can then surprise her with our presence as she adjusts to the new environment we are now experiencing. I think she will like it here, and I know she will be very happy to see us. It will be interesting to meet the other souls who will be looking to rejoin her too—it's then we will know truly what "family" means. We won't take anything for granted then. We will just experience eternal love.

Chapter Six

SHARING STORIES

I glide through the meadow. I have some control over where I go and what soul I see or sense, but I am being presented with different experiences as directed by God. As I move through the green meadow I experience its beauty, but I also experience a feeling of tremendous belonging; I am not a stranger here, even though I've not met many of the souls I'm surrounded by. All of a sudden I am face-to-face—so to speak—with a calico cat. The calico has such a playful demeanor about him. It doesn't look like he takes any of this seriously. His attitude is one of playful enjoyment as he takes every new experience in stride.

I can tell that he hasn't had an easy life. I see the scars imbedded in his soul, and it's as if pain is pouring through his wounds. Yet, somehow, he has covered his scars with "purr-fect" contentment. He's learned to live with what has happened to him, and he has forgiven those who hurt him. I stay still until he becomes aware of my presence. The Calico moves closer. He quietly asks if I know what this place is and why he is here. I tell him and then ask him about his life. He remains silent for a while.

The Calico begins by saying, "I haven't experienced much love in my life. I was born on the street in an inner-city neighborhood. My mother did the best she could for my three siblings and me. Food was scarce and we survived as best we could. Unfortunately, there were some people who grabbed my mother when she was away from us looking for food. They taunted her for fun, and when they were finished, they threw her off a bridge and into a river. We never saw her again." I just listen because I know there are a few cruel people in the world. I also know that there are far more who are indifferent to the suffering of others. They are wrapped up in their own worlds and don't hear the desperation of others while dealing with their own.

He continues, "We survived as best we could. Two of my siblings were run over by a car, and the other one died from hunger. I was able to find someone to take me in. She and her family were kind, and I had enough to eat. I got out of her house one day to explore the outside, but I got lost and couldn't find my way back home. I encountered a big dog who started to growl at me and show his teeth. So I began to run as he started to chase me—I kept running and running out of fear. At some point I realized that I had no way of knowing how to return to the kind family who took me in. This was painful."

I think about my life in the wild. Those of us who aren't domesticated don't have as much to lose as those who are. Perhaps we're better off? Still, we do have to rely on people once in a while, even if it's just to make sure we aren't hurt or in danger. It's nice when we do encounter caring people because then we can rejoin them in this green pasture. It's nice to think that there will be someone who will recognize us when they are directed to this place. I ask the Calico to continue with his story, because I am curious if he has someone to wait for, as I'm still waiting for the woman.

The Calico sighs as he speaks, "I don't have anyone who cared for me after I got lost. I don't know if the woman who took me in would recognize me any longer. I died a year after I lost my way. There were some boys who thought it would be fun to use me as a ball, and they kept tossing me around from person to person. It didn't matter if I was dropped. I would just be picked up again and tossed some more. At some point they got tired of this game and my cries. No one stopped them. No one heard my cries. I gave up struggling and just became limp from lost hope. When they did stop, I lay down curled in a ball. They kicked at me but I didn't move. Then one boy set me on fire. I just laid there in spite of their laughter. I knew this wouldn't take long. Then I heard their laughter no more."

I feel the Calico's pain and am overwhelmed by such a feeling of sorrow. I have never experienced anything like this. I don't know how to respond except to be there quietly for the Calico. I know that there is cruelty in the world, but it's not done on purpose in the animal world. It's done for survival and food, but it's never done for fun. I'm not sure why some people feel the need to be cruel. Perhaps they were treated cruelly themselves, or they were rewarded for hurting lives that were weaker or smaller than they were. I think people call this *bullying*, but it got out of hand in the Calico's case. Could they not see the Calico's pain?

He asks me, "What happens to someone like me who has no one to wait for?"

I reply that I don't know. I look around for the beagle angel I met on my way in; he directed me to where I was to wait, so I am sure he can answer this question. I ask the Calico to stay where he is and I will come back with an answer for him. The beagle angel must've known that I need him, because I turn around and he is there. I explain the Calico's life situation to him.

The beagle angel just smiles. He looks at the Calico and says, "No one is forgotten here. Just as there are pets and animals waiting for the people they loved, there are also people who couldn't have pets for various reasons looking for a pet or animal to love now. All who enter this green pasture of waiting are looking for companionship after years of loneliness or sorrow. It's not just animals, it happens to people too. There are some who are left with no one to genuinely care about them or no one to care for."

I am relieved that everyone is included and cared about. The world holds too much rejection, suffering, and loneliness for some of those living in it. There's uncertainty from day to day for too many. I continue to probe the beagle angel as to how everyone here is recognized and their situations known. I want desperately to comfort the calico, but I myself am new here. Maybe it isn't my purpose to comfort the calico because I am only another imperfect soul?

The beagle angel just smiles and his wings slowly vibrate with excitement as he says, "God knows every soul He created, no matter the bodily form each is given. Every soul goes through experiences in the earthly world. Some of those experiences are pleasant and others not so much. Yet God brings us all home to Him at the appointed time. We arrive back into eternal life with what we've lived with, and God makes us whole once again. God knows the brokenness some carry and pairs souls who can help each other heal. No one is left behind in loneliness and rejection. God draws all toward Himself in a love that is beyond all understanding."

I turn to look at the calico, and then turn back to thank the beagle angel but he has disappeared from view. I go back to the calico and explain everything the beagle angel has told me. The calico is relieved that he will find another human soul to have a caring relationship with.

It isn't just people who couldn't have pets who walk through here—there are others who couldn't have children or a family for whatever reason. There are children who died young and never experienced family, and there are the souls of babies who were never born into the physical world, either because something went wrong in the womb, or because they weren't able to be born for various human reasons, or their birth, through no one's fault, would've endangered their mother.

While I am explaining the reuniting of souls broken through some loss or suffering, the beagle angel joins both of us. The slow movement of his wings continues to provide comfort and a feeling of unity with each other in this green pasture. The beagle angel further explains, "God knows what each imperfect soul has experienced and He brings those together who complete each other's brokenness. It might be from love once experienced, or it might be to experience for the first time what the souls need but was never found on earth. Everyone who arrives here is made whole. God also holds the souls of never-born babies to His heart and never lets them go, because while their purpose on earth was very short-lived, they did have an impact in the world."

The calico and I just stare at each other in disbelief because we can't anticipate what we've not experienced. We can't possibly know what will happen, because we cannot pull from the past to predict the future. We just wait in the green pasture and continue to observe souls coming, reuniting or uniting for the first time, and then walking across the bridge with the rainbow covering it. We can't see what's beyond the bridge, but we know that one day we will. I'm still waiting for the woman who helped me and who I went to see the night I died. I wanted to say goodbye and help her to realize how much she meant to me. I'm glad that I meant something to someone so that they would care about me. It is so important to feel loved so we can give love to others.

As I reminisce about the person I loved on earth, I see the calico floating toward the soul of a never-born baby girl. Both recognize that they are connected in some way, and that God wants them to be together as they both prepare to cross over the Rainbow Bridge. They both need each other and recognize the love that is pulling them together. They are carried toward the Rainbow Bridge by the force of the love that has brought them close in spirit. I watch the process of uniting in and with God's love. I wave to the calico, although I don't know if I'm seen. That's okay because my time will come at some point, and perhaps I'll once again see my feline friend. I'm glad the calico finally found the love in eternity that eluded him while on earth. Maybe one day he will also find the family who loved him before he got lost. All good things come to each of us at the appointed time. I think that's what faith and hope are all about.

Chapter Seven

PLAYFUL PAUSE

I turn around and am in awe of the majestic horse I see coming toward me. I still see her physical presence reflected in her soul. She was quite a powerful horse in her day with her long flowing mane. She looks like she has had a good life, a happy life in the presence of kind people. She exudes joy and a perceptive intuition. She watches others on the green meadow as if taking in their experiences as her own.

She finally turns toward me and I perceive a glistening in her eyes…. or at least the spirituality of what would be her eyes. It seems unlikely that a soul could have eyes, but those of us here haven't completely become fully spiritual beings yet. That will happen as we cross over the Rainbow Bridge to the other side. She playfully asks me how an old toad happened to cross her path. I smile and tell her that it's her lucky day. She lets out a loud neigh as her head leans backward with delight.

I can tell we'll be fast friends. I ask the horse what her story is, if she doesn't mind sharing. She replies that she would be happy to tell me. She begins, "I belonged to a little girl who so desperately wanted a horse. Her father had plenty of land in a rural community, so he set out to find the perfect horse for her. He searched near and far until he found me, a young filly with a gentle temperament. I was only a year old when her dad bought me. The little girl was seven years old, so we grew up together you might say. Oh, how she loved me!"

I smile as I imagine how special this relationship is, evident by the soothing tone of the horse's voice. I ask the horse to continue because I want to learn more about love. I have noticed that love can be given but not always seen by the intended recipient for whatever reason—love can be elusive regarding its desire to be seen. More often than not, it reveals itself through actions toward another. Yes, it can be spoken also, but if there are no actions to sustain it in someone's heart, then the words become empty of meaning.

The horse continues, "The little girl learned how to ride on my back, and she loved the way nature touched her as we traveled throughout the countryside. She learned how to brush me and teach me tricks, which I was happy to perform for her. She made sure I had enough food and water during the day. She would always rush to my side as soon as she got home from school. We were constant companions during the summer, and we rode often. She of course had chores to complete, but I was never far away. I looked out for her just as she did for me."

I enjoy hearing the stories all around me in this pasture. It passes the time while we wait for loved ones to come and find us so we can enter eternal life together. Even those who didn't have the experience of someone loving them during life know that God has someone special for them to love in eternity. There is no time continuum in eternal life. There is no need for time since it's a human concept to set up a routine while we are on earth. Eternity is forever constant with no need to sleep—it just is.

My friend the horse speaks proudly of the little girl she loves, "She became quite an expert horseback rider. We both practiced every chance we got and never tired of each other's company. We participated in quite a few competitions and took first place in some of them. The little girl I love grew up before my very eyes, and I can't understand how the time passed by so quickly. Then came the day when it was time for her to go away to college. Oh, how I missed her! Her father took care of me while she was gone, but it just wasn't the same. However, when she was home over the holidays and during the summer, it was like she had never been gone. We quickly got back into the same joyful routine."

I can only imagine how that felt. It must've been very hard for both of them to have been far apart even for a little while. That being said, there was so much to look forward to as it got closer to the girl coming home from college. It's nice to have been a part of a loving family, this makes all of the difference in the world in how you look at things and how you experience life. When you've known someone is there to take care of you and enjoy being with you, it's easy to develop a strong sense of who you are. I wish I had that, but my life in the wild taught me different things, and I became a survivor for the sake of my own toad family.

I ask the horse to continue, so she begins again. "The girl went to college for many years, as she had decided to become a veterinarian. Of course I was pleased, but I missed her so much. I was getting older and I missed the rides we would take, even though I still saw her on her vacation time and during the summer. I understand what loneliness is, even though I knew she would return each time. I knew she loved me, but it was still difficult to wait for her to return home. Finally she did, and she was able to take care of me in a different way to make sure that I stayed healthy. She had her own practice now so there was less time, but I saw her every day. This was worth the wait!"

I am enthralled listening to how both of them grew into their lives both separately and with each other. The horse's life span is longer than mine because I lived in the wild. I'm taking all of this in as if it was my own experience. This increases my understanding of others—I am seeing how life can be different for everyone even though we might be in the same place at the same time. I guess that's why we can't really judge someone else. If we do, we are only placing them in our own lives rather than seeing them in theirs. That's a powerful lesson.

The horse is anxious to continue and I want to hear more, so I quiet down. She begins again, "My girl got married and began a family of her own. She had a little girl who grew to love me too. I was getting much older, so as this little girl grew, I was a safe horse to ride. I'm proud that she learned to ride me by the time she was five, and that she felt safe with me. Life came full circle for me. I got to spend much time with both of the girls I loved, and it doesn't get better than that. Yet by the time my little girl was ten, I got sick. It became hard for me to breathe and then stand up. It was my time to leave my family, but my girl was right beside me as I passed into where I am now. Everything has a beginning and an end. However, endings always bring new beginnings."

I never thought about things this way because my life contained so much uncertainty. The horse's story shows me how much I've missed. Yet my life was meant to be very different from the way the horse's life was. I'm sure the beagle angel could explain this to me.

Sure enough, as soon as I think this, the beagle angel is right in front of me. I'm amazed at how he knows when I need him without trying to find him. He speaks softly, "God places each of us in different scenarios or life contexts. None of the them are better than another, but there are different purposes for each soul God brings into being on earth. It's not just the purpose for individual souls, but also the interaction of multiple souls to bring about what God is trying to teach those involved. I don't understand God fully, although I've been in eternal life for quite a while. God's intent seems not for me to know or understand, or at least not yet."

The beagle angel goes on to say, "It isn't helpful to compare ourselves with any other soul as each is loved by God as He created them. Some souls may have more opportunity but that doesn't make them better. Some souls may have less but that doesn't make them worse. The important thing is to take what we've been given to work with and make something out of that. What we create for ourselves and others is of our own choosing, and it starts with the decisions each soul makes every moment of every day. A soul who has received little can create much good if it chooses. Likewise, a soul who has received much can choose to enjoy it selfishly rather than develop it for the common good. It's all about how we use the free will God gave each soul. Choose well on earth, because it's what you carry with you into eternal life."

I had never looked at life in quite this way. I just took each moment as it happened, with no plan from one day to the next. I had a simple soul as an old toad, and a simple life, but I did have an impact on the woman who noticed me. I could sense that she cared about me. It was her caring that made me want to stay close by, and I wanted my family to know that her property was a safe place to be. We always found our way into her window wells only to discover that we couldn't jump out. I'm so glad that her dog alerted her to our presence so that she began to look for us. She rescued many of my family. That's how I knew she would see me when I wanted to say goodbye. I took a leap of faith, so to speak.

All of a sudden, I see my horse friend become very alert. She fills with emotion as she looks toward the gate, filled with joy. I watch her to see what will happen next. She starts moving quickly so I turn to see what catches her attention. I see her! It is the woman she spent most of her life with! Time doesn't exist in heaven so I can't tell how long time kept them apart. She likewise catches her eye as she looks around. The beagle angel had led her toward a particular spot in the meadow.

Both embrace with soul-filled joy, and I can't look away from this blessed experience of true love. They just take each other in, as those who've not seen each other for a while do. They join their souls together never to be separated again. They spend moments conversing without words as they slowly walk toward the bridge with the rainbow over it. I watch as they became less and less visible. As they reach the bridge, they both turn to look back at the pasture where my horse friend had waited for her loved one.

Finally, my horse friend catches sight of me and bows down on one front leg and raises her head to the sky with his mane flowing freely. She gives out a loud neigh as if to show me how happy and thankful she is. Then she looks at her girl, whose time has come to join her, and they face the rainbow. I see the rainbow glow warmly, and as they both hold on to each other they allow the rainbow to pull them across the bridge ever so slowly so as not to diminish what they are experiencing. What they feel now will never end. Once they reach the rainbow, I see their souls merge into a mist that dissipates as they move through to the other side of the Rainbow Bridge. Their journey is complete.

I am overcome by emotion as I understand the meaning of love more fully. The beagle angel is there to comfort me because each reunion of souls into eternal life is so beautiful to witness. He also tells me that when my turn comes, I will once again see those I've met in the green pasture in eternal life. So we all will continue to experience the flow of life in its spiritual form as death in life is just as important as birth. Death allows us to be free from our physical bodies, which hold us back. Death is a process where we enter and emerge into the splendor of life eternal, where we are with God and those we have loved in life.

Yes, that applies to every life because each life, no matter which physical body God has placed a soul into, has meaning and value to God. Each soul returns home when God says it's time to come home. Our final home is our forever home. We've been there before, but once we are placed into a developing physical body we are born a clean slate with no memory of the eternal home we left. Each angel knows that this is the mystery of life.

So God gives every living being a guardian angel who looks out for us while on earth, who watches over us and protects our souls. Without free will there can be no love. However, the choices we make aren't always the best. God understands this because only He is perfect. We learn through our choices and the impact they have not only on us, but those around us. When we cross the Rainbow Bridge with our loved ones, we regain our understanding as God reveals Himself once again. We are forgiven and made whole as we see who we truly are. We're home.

Chapter Eight

BRIDGE IN THE DISTANCE

I see a newcomer floating toward me with a determined yet playful look. Then all of a sudden, he becomes like a flash of light moving from side to side, and then in circles, back and forth. The souls around the green pasture closest to me are moving closer to each other and in one direction. Wow!! The newcomer is a border collie and he's doing his best to herd the other animal souls into one place. They are listening to him or at least trying to get out of his way. The border collie has this energy that seems to have its own gravitational pull, as any true leader would have. The souls being herded know that there is a good surrounding them rather than a danger, and they playfully laugh.

I observe that everyone is calm and their closeness to one another is comforting. They begin to play games with the border collie, and he doesn't mind when he has to go after strays. He smiles and surrounds them with his energy. This activity creates a positive experience for all involved while they wait for their family members to join them. It's fun to watch!

When everyone takes a break, I approach the border collie. I want to hear his story and see what I can learn from his life experiences. He looks at me and is also curious as to who I am, because I'm not an animal he would consider herding. That doesn't mean he won't try!

I begin the conversation by commenting that he seems to instantly feel very comfortable here. The border collie responds,

"Yes, I am. I experienced quite a bit of heaven on earth with my second family. However, I do feel sad that I lost my first family. We had all taken a vacation, and when we stopped for a rest, my nose got the better of me. I started following the wide variety of scents, and I couldn't make my way back to my family—I was lost. I always missed the children I never saw again, and I'm sure they were sad that they couldn't find me." The beagle angel told him that perhaps he'll find them here at some point?"

I also feel sad because his regret of getting lost in his immediate pleasure changed the course of his life. It's funny how we all have regrets, but some of our choices can have life-changing consequences. We never know what could've been or what will be, so it can be scary.

I ask him what happened next and he gets very quiet for a while. He then continues, "I was picked up by animal control as I was looking for food any place I could smell it. This was a good thing because it was cold and rainy, and now I had a warm place to stay. However, I missed my family so much."

I am quiet because I had never really known a family outside of my toad family. At least not until the woman moved into the neighborhood. I try to imagine the loss of those I loved but had gotten separated from. I imagine always looking for them and hopefully finding them someday. Still, the border collie found others to love him just as much. That is amazing!

The border collie continues to share his story. He says with a smile, "I was in an outside kennel and I watched everyone who approached to look at me. There was one couple whom I sensed had kind hearts, so I walked to the front of the kennel, wagged my tail, and showed them I was interested in them. However, as soon as another couple came up alongside of them, I walked away and sat down with my back to them. I made it clear that I wasn't interested in the second couple. As soon as that second couple left, I walked back to the front of the pen. They didn't adopt me that day, but I heard their discussion that they were interested. I was pleased."

The border collie notes that he was beginning to get sick when they came back for him the next day. There had been cold rains for the last week, and he couldn't find warmth before he was brought to the animal shelter. He says, "They brought me home and I progressively got worse. It was a Sunday, but in those days there weren't any emergency veterinary clinics. They called around to see if any veterinarian would come in on a Sunday to examine me, and they finally found one."

He continues, "I was at the animal hospital and a chest x-ray was taken. I had a pneumonia. I was panting heavily and shaking. I couldn't breathe well, and I couldn't keep warm. They also found out that I had worms, but I would have to come back for treatment of that once I recovered from pneumonia. My new family was given an antibiotic, and we went home. They took very good care of me. I had enough food and a warm place to sleep. When I was well enough to jump on the bed, they didn't even mind if I joined them for mutual warmth."

That intrigues me. I had never slept with a human, let alone inside of a house. It must be amazing! All animals love contact with others, both spiritual and physical. I want to mention emotional also, but wild animals tend not to form this bond unless there is some special human who interacts with them in some way when they need help. While they don't become a part of our lives for very long, we do recognize their care for us. We repay their kindness by keeping watch from a distance. We talk with the other wild animals to let them know these are people friendly to us, especially the wild animals who in their nature might attack them. Those of us who've been shown respect by humans send out messages to all of the animal kingdom to safeguard them.

The border collie starts looking around to make sure no soul has ventured away from the group. It's a sixth sense, so to speak, of just knowing when to find someone who's at risk of being lost. That's funny, given that his own spirit of adventure allowed his nose to draw him away from his first family. Still, it shows that he's more concerned about others than he is for himself. That's a very unselfish trait in today's world, but there are those—human and animal—who know that we are all part of God's creation. We need to look out for each other and prevent harm when we can.

Then suddenly the border collie turns his gaze toward me. I smile and communicate that I'm still part of his group, even though I want to spend some time understanding about his life and what drives him. He smiles in return and allows me to be next to him.

"What have you learned?" I ask him.

He takes a deep breath and appears to go deep into thought. Finally, he says, "There's both good and bad in every form of life. However, there is a tendency for humans to disconnect with nature and the earth they live on. Both need to be respected, just as with any other relationship, because God connected everything for the benefit of all in order to survive."

He continues, "It seems animals never worry about having enough because their souls know that God will provide. Humans' high level of thought leads them to worry, so they begin to accumulate much more in money and material things than they will ever need. The problem with this is everything on earth is limited. So excessive accumulation by some leaves less available for others to live on and enjoy. This creates poverty for some, if those who accumulate beyond their needs don't share some of their wealth to help others in some way. Sharing wealth could be seen as an investment in the future, because it gives those with less of a chance to get an education or a skill, or even open a business. This not only helps them but also their families build a future. The couple who adopted me shared some of what they had to allow me to survive. I showed my gratitude by giving them my love and loyally watching out for them."

I have never thought of this before. I was just concerned with my daily needs, which included helping my own family survive. When I thought about the woman who rescued me, I could begin to catch a glimpse of what the border collie was explaining. However, most of my life was being in the survival-of-the-fittest mode. Many humans function in that mode too, so we have much in common while we're living on earth. Over time though, some begin to recognize, just as I did, that when we care about others, there is always enough. Our loving God always provides for us when we give to others out of our excess.

I am so enthralled in what the border collie is doing and sharing that I don't see the beagle angel behind us. He is observing both of us very quietly and smiles with approval when we notice him. I introduce the border collie to him, and the border collie looks like he would like to herd the beagle angel. He is looking at the angel wings pulsating and wondering what purpose they serve. The border collie gets closer to sniff them, but stops short of touching the wings.

The beagle angel goes on to explain, "Here at the Rainbow Bridge is a playful time while we wait for our loved ones. There are many different souls here, each with a different purpose in God's creation. Once we cross the Rainbow Bridge into eternal life, our purpose is not only fulfilled but united with God's plan for us within the tapestry of life coming full circle."

The border collie sits at attention and allows himself to be guided by the beagle angel's thoughts. He is pleased. It seems to him that God is herding all waiting souls to enter eternity toward Him. He asks the beagle angel if God is a border collie.

The beagle angel smiles and continues, "No, God has no form and yet God can become a form just like He did in His son. God is an infinite being yet He sends souls to earth as finite beings in order teach us how to be like Him in some way. Suffering on earth can be painful, like when you were separated from your first family. Yet it can be a great teacher if we bring God into it to guide us through it. Sometimes it is the suffering soul that is learning the lessons of life, and at other times the people who come to the aid of those who suffer are the ones who learn compassion, kindness, and the keys to their own suffering."

The border collie pauses for a few minutes to think about this. Then he turns away from the beagle angel and faces the other animal souls waiting to cross the Rainbow Bridge. The border collie sighs knowingly and says, "We're all alike. The suffering of each of us may be different, but the way to get past it is to go through it with each other together as God meant us to be. Someday we will get to experience what it's like on the other side of the bridge with our loved ones by our side. I can't imagine the perfect joy I will feel once I'm in God's presence forever."

The beagle angel just smiles because he isn't allowed to talk about eternity. This is a time of waiting. Once God calls souls to come over the Rainbow Bridge, they will experience the wonder of seeing Him close as He welcomes them home never to be separated again. Then each of us will experience the rewards of passing through suffering while keeping our souls safe from harm. Joy will be perfect with the God who loves us.

As we enjoy the meadow, the beagle angel nods to the border collie and asks, "Do you want to wait for your couple, or would you like to cross the Rainbow Bridge and see them later?"

The border collie says, "I have to wait for one of them at least." Just as he says this, a man walks up to him and smiles. The border collie starts running around him and finally jumps up to him.

The man asks the border collie if he wants to wait for his better half or go ahead and walk across. The border collie says in reply, "I know we will quickly find her when she arrives, so let's go across the bridge and explore what's on the other side. Maybe I can find some souls to herd in eternal life? She would want us to have fun while we wait for her."

The man agrees. This time the border collie will not lose a loved one.

God always attaches the bonds of love to the souls that He has meant to be together. Border collies always find their way back to those they love while in Heaven.

Chapter Nine

THE TUNNEL

I am watching outside of heaven's gates as animals come out of the tunnel. There is this very intelligent-looking cat who is very sophisticated. She has bright eyes and cautiously looks around the mysterious place she finds herself in. The beagle angel is sitting patiently waiting for her to glide toward the lion and the lamb. Both of them are watching her quite intently. The Siamese cat is taking her time being fickle as she notices everything around her. It is almost as if she is looking for something worthy of a hunt. She would enjoy a chase right about now.

Finally, she sees the lion. "Oh my!" she says. She notices the lion is patiently waiting until he caught her attention. She stops and sits down five feet in front of him all the while gazing intently at him. The lion roars a welcome to her. The Siamese just lays down, stretches, and then yawns. After several minutes, she meows back. She isn't impressed by the lion even if his size is intimidating. She will hold her ground and pretend he is just another cat. This is better than a hunt in her mind.

She isn't too interested in the lamb because she wants a challenge and the lamb is very meek. The lion, on the other hand, is ready to put her in her place. That amuses her. She will toy with him until she gets tired of the game, knowing that he will keep staring his dominant look.

I call to the Siamese cat from just within the gate, and I invite her to come over to where I am.

She looks surprised to see an American toad in her vicinity and she says, "What are you doing here? I used to hunt your species just for fun."

I ask her if she knows where she is and she replies tersely, "No." She looks at the lion and starts to slowly walk past him while keeping a steady gaze. Then she tickles his nose with her tail and meanders through the gates.

She looks at me with amusement, then suddenly looks past me. The beagle angel is hovering behind me, slowly vibrating her wings. The Siamese asks her what those floppy things are.

The beagle angel replies with a smile, "These are what I have earned in eternity as part of how pleasing my life on earth was to God. My wings reflect the goodness of God, and I use them to direct souls to where they need to be to find their loved ones when their time comes."

The Siamese wonders about who she will look for, because while she was pampered and had everything she could ever want, she never really felt that she was loved. She knows that she will have to think about love and if there was anyone in her life who reflected that.

I feel sad for her because she seems to be feeling lonely and confused in spite of looking confident. I'm moving toward her to ask her what her life was like. She looks my way and taps her paw saying it's okay to approach her.

She is more serious now as I say, "I'm interested in knowing what your life was like. Mine was very hard, living outside year-round with no one to care for me except my other toad family members. Toward the end of my earthly life, I did meet a woman who would rescue our baby toads when they were trapped in a window well. She was concerned they would die because they couldn't get out when the summer sun beat down on them.

"Then one day I decided to jump into the window well myself to meet her. I waited and, sure enough, she saw me. She went to get the small shovel and placed it near where I could jump onto it. She lifted me up and gently placed me in the shade. I was very grateful to her for showing me what love in action could mean for another life. I didn't live much longer than this because I was an old toad, but I finally experienced love in knowing that I was valued. I'll never forget her for that, and she's the one I'm waiting for."

The Siamese continues to stare at me. She begins slowly, "I've always been taken care of and every need I've had was continuously met. I've never had to suffer or fend for myself. I've never lacked food or warmth or any creature comforts. I've never had to meet life's challenges, so I create my own in the form of games. I've never known suffering or loss, and I've never had to find my way back home after getting lost or stolen. My earthly life was picture perfect. It was too perfect, because I've never had to strive for anything. I relied on everything I was given, rather than needing to become independent. So, when I find myself here surrounded by unfamiliar sights, sounds, and souls, I don't know how to react or feel."

I look at her but I don't know what to say. My life was the opposite of hers, yet here we are sitting together in the same place. I think for a moment and then ask, "Who will you wait for here? There must be someone you would like to cross the Rainbow Bridge with?"

She replies with a tear in her eye, "I don't know. I had a nice family, but they were so busy all of the time. They would have someone come in to feed me if they travelled and then would pet me when they came home, but for the most part I entertained myself. Some would call me a self-soother."

The Siamese continues, "Some children learn to do this in order to adapt to being left alone. It's not that we're unloved, but rather it's that the expression of love is always for someone else and not us. I didn't really experience the warmth of being held and spoken to softly, or of having my fur stroked lovingly. I've never felt that closeness of someone who really sees me for who I am and accepts me unconditionally. It sounds like I'm lonely in the midst of others, and I guess I am."

I listen closely. I sit quietly with the Siamese cat for a few minutes deep in thought. Then I ask again, "Who do you think you will wait for? Is there no one who thought you were special?"

She doesn't respond for a while, and then she says, "No, I don't think there's anyone. The greatest loneliness is experienced when you are surrounded by others yet no one notices you or what you're feeling. So I find myself in this wonderful place, but I can't experience the joy of being here, because there's no one I look forward to seeing when their time comes."

I am not aware that the beagle angel is listening to our conversation, but his job is to direct all souls toward the path they're supposed to be walking on. Beagle angel speaks gently to the Siamese and says, "I see you for who you really are. God has shown me all of your soul's life imprints and where your experiences are lacking. Not everyone who arrives in the meadow by the Rainbow Bridge has someone who's been special in their earthly life. So, when there's no one to fill the shoes of walking hand in hand into eternity, I wait until someone arrives who also doesn't have anyone special. When the soul arrives who lacks the complement of one who's waiting, I bring them together so no one is alone."

The beagle angel looks off in the distance. An unborn baby is at the gate, looking lost and in pain. This little soul wasn't given the chance of life for whatever reason because the placenta detached in the womb. Human nature isn't perfect and sometimes mothers lose their babies through no fault of their own. God understands. The beagle angel guides the tiny soul over to the Siamese and says, "This little baby soul didn't experience life on earth except for a short time in the womb. He was separated from his mother before he had a chance to experience the love she had to offer."

The beagle angel continues, "You, on the other hand, experienced all of the pleasures and experiences life had to offer as a pampered Siamese cat. You are looking for unconditional love and this tiny soul also needs maternal love. You know what you would want to feel about love, and this unborn soul can love unconditionally because he isn't tarnished by the suffering of the world he would have experienced if born. The two of you can give each other what you need, and this bond can be as strong as any true loving relationship on earth. Your maternal instincts will guide you. Please join each other in God's love as it is time for both of you to walk across the Rainbow Bridge. God is waiting for both of you to join Him."

I am amazed at how no one is lost as I watch them go. The beagle angel knows so much about the process of life on earth, the heavenly gates waiting area, and eternal life. He truly is a beacon directing everyone onto the path they are supposed to be on. I am experiencing much here, but there is so much more to learn. The beagle angel is still next to me, so I ask, "Is anyone truly lost?"

He replies, "No, only a very few and it's because they've turned away from God and sinned against His Holy Spirit. No matter what has happened on earth, souls return to eternal life. God brings them home after they've gone through the purpose intended for them."

He continues, "Even the unborn who have not had a chance to live return, although the gifts they were given by God to share with those on earth never came into fruition. So, if the soul carrying the cure for cancer is never born, the cure is delayed. If the unborn soul carrying the solution to avoid nuclear holocaust is never born, the risk of complete annihilation escalates. We each have a gift to bring to others, but even sharing that can be delayed depending upon the choices each of us make with the free will God has given us. Yet there can be no love without free will, because we have to choose to accept love. It cannot be forced upon us."

I keep these conversations within my soul. They comfort me, and I know everything will come together at some point. Life is complicated, especially because each soul has its own journey through earthly life and then back home to eternal life with God. Time also changes, at least how we think of it. When we're young, it seems like it will take forever for things to happen. However, as we get older, time speeds up and life begins to appear more finite. The beagle angel tells me that there is no concept of time in eternal life, so perhaps time moves quicker and quicker to the point where time just stands still? I have to wait until I cross the Rainbow Bridge to find out.

Chapter Ten

THE WILD

Carina Chock

The turtle casually and methodically crossed the road. It's not in his nature to rush, even as he caught sight of a fast-approaching car. The turtle reacted to his fright in the only way he can, which is to withdraw into his shell. The driver did see the turtle and rode over the shell without hitting it, but he was traveling so fast that the turtle spun upside down on his shell and glided to the side of the road. Upside down, he contemplates his predicament. "I'll need a little help with this situation," he said. So he waited until someone noticed him.

The turtle stayed upside down all night and tried to make the best of keeping warm. At least it wasn't raining, because a downpour would bring enough rain quickly to partially flood his shell. He woke up to the sound of singing birds, for which he was grateful. Once the turtle stuck his head outside and saw that the sun was shining, he was even more grateful. He tried with all of his energy to flip himself over, but all he could do was rock back and forth. "Oh well," he said with resignation. There was nothing else he could do but wait.

The turtle had fallen back to sleep when he felt a gentle kick to his shell. He carefully stuck his head out to see if it was someone friendly or someone who meant him harm—these days you can never be so sure. It was a young, curious boy, so the turtle stuck out his four legs too. Then he moved his head and legs about to show the boy that he wasn't able to right himself. The boy smiled, bent down, and grabbed hold of his shell on both sides. He flipped the turtle over and then touched his front leg. The turtle was very grateful.

The boy got up and continued walking. He had to get to school. The boy turned back to the turtle and told him, "I will be back after school's out. You're probably hungry so you may not be here when I return, but if you are I'll bring you home and give you a place to safely wander around on my grandparents' farm." The turtle was touched by his kindness and smiled as the boy walked away. This made such a difference in uplifting the turtle's spirits, doing things to help all others, including animals, because we are all connected.

I see the turtle walk slowly out of the tunnel. He is somewhat disoriented and doesn't know where he is or how he got here by Heaven's Gate. I see him approaching as I am standing inside the meadow by the gate. Once he is cleared by the lion and the lamb, and guided in by the beagle angel, I have a chance to talk to him. The story you just heard is what he told me with sadness. It wasn't the kindness of the young boy which had affected him, but rather that he didn't get a chance to see him again.

The turtle speaks softly, "While I was trying to cross the road to find something to eat and drink, I was run over by a large truck. Once I left my body, I did see that it was completely crushed by the weight of the truck. Other vehicles ran over me too as people were too distracted to even notice my body was there. I was able to remain long enough to see that the boy saw me on his way back from school. He was sad to find me this way, and he shed a few tears as he respectfully picked my body up and brought me to a quiet place to bury me. I'll never forget this young boy's compassion and respect for life!"

I am amazed at the kindness of a boy so young! Compassion is so important for creating happiness on earth. I think the human phrase is "random act of kindness." Some parents try to limit the experience their children have of suffering, thinking that avoidance will help them grow into more emotionally strong adults. However, it's through the experience of suffering that children learn what it feels like to walk in other people's shoes, and what behavior causes hurt to others. Suffering is hard to endure, but it teaches empathy, compassion, resilience, self-reliance, and a sense of responsibility, just to name a few.

I watch the turtle move around the meadow with a sense of dejection. He sees the other souls playing games or exploring their environment as they wait for loved ones, but he suspects his wait will be a long one. He is all alone and moving about listlessly, encapsulated in his own grief. I watch as the beagle angel moves toward him at a slow pace. When he is close by, the beagle angel faces the turtle, smiling yet saying nothing. Both stare at each other for the longest time, not moving. Finally, the beagle angel instructs the turtle to follow him. The turtle reluctantly does so.

They end up at a smaller secluded section of the meadow, and the beagle angel gently asks the turtle to look in the distance. The turtle lifts his head, and he sees a pond filled with all kinds of turtles. His spirits lift tremendously as he strolls over to visit with his soul-turtles. They all look toward him as he approaches. When he reaches them, they all encircle him and move slowly around him so they can introduce themselves. It is a joyous moment and the turtle looks back at the beagle angel with gratitude. The turtle sees that there are others like himself, and he is welcome in their midst.

I move to where the beagle angel is, and we look at each other with a knowing glance of how important reaching out to others is. I am very happy for the turtle because he feels loved. I ask the beagle angel why he interacted with the turtle so early upon his arrival in the meadow, because I notice that he usually waits until the new souls have a chance to explore the meadow. He says, "Sometimes a soul is so beaten down from their experiences on earth that they arrive immobilized and unable to reach out to anyone to get what they need. Whereas on earth they may never find a friend to give them a sense of direction and well-being, no soul is left on its own once it is close to the presence of God. God won't allow it because He values every soul he creates. Everyone is loved unconditionally and no one is judged by other souls."

The beagle angel continues, "I try to ease the pain of souls who've almost never known a time without suffering. I take a look at what they need and I direct them to others they can relate too. Every time I do this, the suffering soul is filled with new hope and a desire to want to go on. It's so important for every soul to find like souls who are kindred spirits, because it's through their connection with others that their God-given gifts are energized and circulated through God's creation, of which we are all a part. We need each other, but so often self-serving desires get in the way of truly being in communion with each other. However, when those desires are set aside for the good of all, communities thrive. There's a strong similarity between the words *communion* and *community*, don't you think?"

As the beagle angel leaves, I continue to watch the turtle with his kindred souls. He is happy now that he found other turtle souls. It doesn't stop there because he finds the strength to reach out to other species' souls. He sees many types of frogs, ducks, geese, chipmunks, and even a few majestic swans. They all smile back and acknowledge his presence. He begins to feel accepted, and because of this he is able to accept others, even though they are very different from him. It's because of these differences that they learn many new perspectives and ways of looking at their surroundings. It is a way of surviving for all of them, because no one has all of the answers, but with all of their different ways of looking at things they always find a solution to whatever they are facing.

The turtle sees me watching his interaction with his newfound companions. He begins to move toward me with a smile. His soul is much lighter in spirit now and he appears more joyful and complete. He tells me that he is happy that the beagle angel took him under his wing and directed him to where he needs to be. "This must be similar to prayers being answered," he says. He speaks further, "We need something desperately but can't find what we need, so we ask God for it. We don't know how God will answer or when, but we patiently wait, knowing that our prayers have been heard. The beagle angel brought the answer to a happier life for me."

I explain to the turtle, "No one knows who will come along and help change our lives for the better, so it's best not to despair if there are no immediate answers. Prayers are answered, but God chooses the best time to reveal His response. It's best not to hold on too tight to what we think we want or need, because sometimes God gives us something that is not only different but ultimately better and more healing for our souls."

The turtle asks me if I think he will see the young boy again.

"Most definitely!" I reply with enthusiasm. I continue, "He loves you as proven by his actions. Love never dies because it is eternal and never forgotten. When we truly love others, its bonds are unbreakable. Unconditional love is eternal and never ending. So never be afraid to love and do good for others, because that's what will come back to you when you are in need."

He thanks me and starts back toward those who treat him like family. I can tell that he is waiting with expectant faith for the young boy who helped him. I don't explain to the turtle that time in the meadow, just like the concept of time in eternal life, is not the same as on earth. Twenty years on earth can seem like a few minutes here. I don't know when God will decide to bring them back together again, but I do know that they will never be separated again.

None of us knows what God thinks or feels or when He plans to bring together all of the threads that are part of the tapestry of His creation. We just know that each of us plays a small part in the totality of what our Creator has set in motion. So it doesn't make sense for one thread to say that it doesn't want to be next to another thread, or that the threads in my group should all be the same color, or that all threads should form the same pattern I'm in. That's not our decision because we aren't the Creator of all that we know as life itself. Each of us needs to be the best soul we were meant to be so the harmony of life will flow without hindrance or obstacles.

All of a sudden, I emerge from being deep in thought, almost as if I am suddenly awakening from a dream. Standing next to me is the once-young boy. He's looking off in the distance toward the pond. The beagle angel directed him to this place while I was thinking. He keeps watching his beloved turtle. Both souls become aware of each other's presence and their bonds of love begin to pull them closer to each other. Ever so slowly they move toward each other, giving them moments to fully realize that they are together again. Finally, they face each other. Both nod simultaneously in agreement that they are ready for their final journey toward the Rainbow Bridge.

So they begin to slowly move away from where I am. I watch, knowing that my time will also come when I see the woman. As they approach the Rainbow Bridge, I see clouds beginning to form over the bridge. Soon they become very dense to greet the turtle and the once-young boy. As their souls reach the bridge entrance and they begin to cross, they are immersed within the clouds. It becomes indistinguishable to tell the difference between them and the clouds as they walk to the other side of the bridge into eternal life.

Someday I will know what eternal life is like. The beagle angel says that it's not his place to explain that to me, because God determines how different souls blend into eternal life. All that I know is that one day each soul will become like God, never to be separated from His love, which surpasses all understanding. I look forward to experiencing this someday, but I will continue to learn from others until the appointed time. We are all one.

Chapter Eleven

BIRDS OF A FEATHER

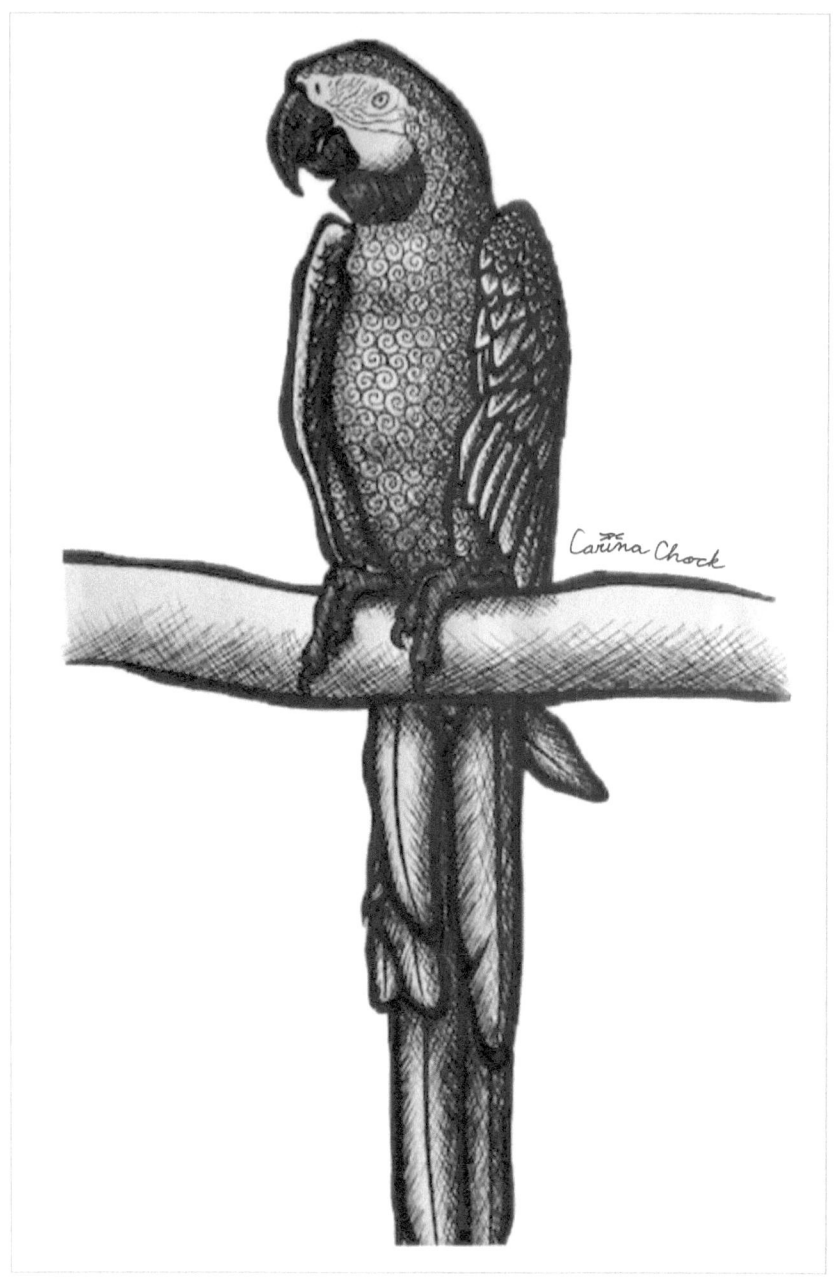

B ecause I am experiencing many souls entering through the gates leading to the Rainbow Bridge, I am suddenly given a great gift: God allows me to see a situation when someone is close to the time of their passing into eternal life. I don't know why this particular time is important for me to observe, but I'm sure I'll discover the reason at some point. I'm in awe as to why an old toad is allowed to see so much wonder. It's almost as if the beagle angel has taken me under his wing to share the eternal wonder I am experiencing.

An old woman sat on her rocker and looked toward her parrot. She smiled but remained silent, knowing that her pet was waiting for a cue to bellow out a phrase.

Finally, the woman said, "What's your name?"

The parrot replied, "My name is Help."

The woman asked, "What does Help do?"

The parrot said without hesitation, "Help watches over you."

The woman smiled with contentment because she was with someone she loved. She didn't think of her parrot as just a bird, but rather another soul who was able to communicate with her. The parrot was good company.

I keep watching and saw as the woman gets up from her rocker and grabbed her white cane. She tapped it in front of her to make sure there were no obstacles in her way as she proceeded to the kitchen of her small apartment. It was time for lunch.

The parrot squawked his delight, "Help is on the way!"

A caregiver visited several times a week to help with food prep, cleaning, laundry, and bathing. So the woman's lunch was in the fridge wrapped nicely, and the parrot's food was right on top of it. The parrot flew to a chair and landed on top of the seatback, as he waited for his meal. He flapped his wings ever so slightly in delight!

The woman laid the dish down on the table in front of the parrot and asked, "What do you say?"

The parrot responded, "Thank you for my food. You are a good friend."

The woman sat down next to the parrot and both began to eat. The parrot ate slowly so as to keep pace with his beloved owner.

Both took their time enjoying their meal and their company. They talked back and forth, with the woman taking the lead and the parrot responding. It was an amazing lifetime of training the parrot to be able to recognize certain cues and situations. For you see, the woman was blind and might someday experience an emergency.

The parrot knew very well how to get help. He could dial "911," open the door and knock on a neighbor's apartment door, or press the woman's emergency button she wore around her neck should she fall or become unresponsive. The parrot had gone through all of the questions and responses many times, and had quite a large vocabulary. It was good for both of them. The woman kept her mind active, and the parrot was engaged in learning way beyond what most parrots have been given the chance to do. Theirs was a very healthy symbiotic relationship filled with love and compassion.

Some blind people have a seeing eye dog, but this old woman chose her own path with the parrot she loved. The woman was so very grateful that her nephew was willing to take her beloved parrot whenever she passed away, because it hurt to think her parrot would have nowhere to go and would also die of a broken heart. If she died in her parrot's presence then she knew he would better understand why she was gone. She knew her time was soon, and she was becoming weaker at eighty-seven. It was getting harder to get around in the dark world caused by her blindness.

She was getting tired of remaining on earth, although she never tired of being with her parrot. She headed off to bed. She said her prayers, which always included her parrot. She turned to Help and asked him if he would remember her.

He replied as she had trained him, "I will never forget you. I love you."

She told him that she loved him too and that they would be together always because of the love that binds them.

I saw the parrot drop his head when he saw that the old woman had died during the night. He flew near her and rested his feathers on her heart and his head on her eyes. He let out a cry of sorrow and then remained with her in silence for a few minutes.

Just as he had been trained, the parrot pressed the medic alert button and notified the dispatcher that the old woman had died. Her nephew arrived around the same time as the undertaker. The police had to be notified also per procedure. The nephew gathered up Help's things, put him in his cage, and they left his aunt's apartment. Help would be well taken care of until his time also came. Both were sad, but they knew the old woman was no longer suffering. She left both of them wonderful memories to cherish.

My attention turns back to the waiting area of the Rainbow Bridge. The beagle angel was watching me while I was deep in thought. I look up and he motions to look toward the gate that souls enter through. My soul eyes open wide as I see the old woman waiting to enter where I am.

I turn to the beagle angel, and I say, "How can this be? Her parrot hasn't died yet!"

The beagle angel thinks for a moment and replies, "Sometimes the bonds of love are so strong that God allows a pet's family member to remain here until their beloved animal joins them. Then they will cross the Rainbow Bridge together to meet other loved ones who've died before them."

I think this is the kindest thing to do. Love is respected in eternal life and it is the most powerful thing there is to unite us. I meet the old woman once she walks past the gate. She can see now and is healed in every way. She looks so young as she smiles at me. Part of her knows that I was there with her and Help. She thinks of her parrot kindly; she misses him, yet she knows he will do very well without her. She finds a rock by a tree and watches all of the other bird souls. They are happily chirping and she feels content.

The beagle angel comes over to her and asks her if she would like to be able to keep an eye on Help. She beams, "Oh, yes!"

So the beagle angel takes her over to a cloud where everything is translucent, and with the love in her soul she is able to focus on Help. He appears sad even though her nephew takes very good care of him. Help has everything he needs. Her nephew was even thoughtful enough to bring home another parrot to try to ease Help's feeling of loss. Yes, animals do have feelings and experience the ups and downs of emotions just as people do. That's why the love that binds humanity and animal-kind is so strong.

I go over to the old woman and ask, "Why did you pick a parrot to help you?"

She replies, "I could've chosen a dog or just used a cane, but I could train a parrot to say words people would understand if I fell or got injured... or died. Since I wanted to continue to live alone once I lost my sight, I needed to find some way to make that work. So, I found a young parrot who hadn't learned words or phrases, which I would have to reverse. It worked out quite well actually, and Help was good company. I named my parrot *Help* because when he alerted people, the first word out of his mouth would be "help." This got people's attention quickly. I then explained this to my neighbors, my nephew, and emergency services."

I just look at her in amazement! This woman is one of the few people I've encountered who realizes that all animals are aware of the human presence, and if people respect us then we respect them. I watch through the cloud with her as she sends waves of love to Help with her soul. She wants him to know that she hasn't left him, and that he's very much in her thoughts. She hopes he can tell that he's not alone, but is continuously surrounded by those who love him forever. She continues to watch over her parrot while she also looks around the meadow to see what other animals are waiting. She sees a few people in the distance, and she decides to take a stroll.

The old woman walks over to those waiting for their pets to join them. She says, "Hello." Everyone looks and smiles. She continues, "How long have all of you been waiting?"

One of the women replies, "It varies for each of us. However, the sorrow of having to entrust our beloved pets to others is something we all share. We not only miss them, but we hope they are taken care of in the manner we all did."

The old woman shakes her head yes, because her parrot grew up under her guidance and she knew how to read what he wanted.

The old woman sits down with them and feels the comfort of their presence. The beagle angel glides over to them and sits down among them as well. He knows it is difficult to wait. He asks them, "Do each of you want to wait here, or would you rather walk over the Rainbow Bridge, and I can send your beloved pet or animal across once they arrive in the meadow?"

They all simultaneously reply, "I'll wait here!"

The beagle angel smiles because he knew they would remain. He looks at the old woman and says gently, "Help will be coming soon."

The old woman smiles in gratitude.

I move back to the gate although I don't know why I am compelled to at that moment. Time is not a factor here in the meadow once each of us walks past the gate. When souls are in their earthly form, the perception of time changes. When someone is young and the body is quick, time seems to move ever so slowly and the wait is long. Then during adulthood, the busyness makes time pass, although things are handled and we somehow fit everything into our schedules nicely.

However, as we get much older, we can't keep up the way we used to. The body slows down but the perception of times speeds up. We look back and all of a sudden can't understand how we got to be so old. Even if we've lived a full life and have many memories to look back on, it just seems to have flown by so quickly. Perhaps that is why by the time we get to heaven, it feels like there is no time and everything stands still. We're out of our bodies and our souls have no physical restrictions to bind us. There's no need to sleep, so there's no sense of being awake. There are no circadian rhythms, no brain waves, and no heartbeats. We just exist and we lose our concept of time—it serves no purpose.

So I mingle and wait for my journey across the Rainbow Bridge. I observe the beagle angel moving toward the gate. All of sudden I see a spectrum of colors and hear a squawk and the word "Help." The old woman's parrot is here to find her.

The beagle angel tells the parrot to follow him. They move away from the gate, and I follow at a distance. The parrot is somewhat afraid because he doesn't understand what is happening. They look at each other as the beagle angel's wings start to slowly move. They continue further as the wings start to move more quickly, and when the beagle angel's wings are in full propulsion speed, the older woman looks up, knowing this is the moment she's been waiting for. The parrot flies as quickly as he can to the woman, their eyes locked on each other.

The parrot finally reaches the old woman and puts his head on her shoulder. He says, "Help is here."

She strokes him and gently pulls him toward her. The woman cries out, "I've missed you so much, Help, but I was watching you from this meadow to make sure you were okay. I've always loved you and you were my precious companion while we were on earth."

The parrot replies, "You took me in and taught me wonderful words. We had something very special and we still do."

The old woman smiles because she knows that love is all that truly matters in the end, because that's all we take with us when we leave our bodies.

The beagle angel approaches them and says, "It is time for both of you to journey further into eternal life. Please cross the Rainbow Bridge where you both will be led to your places in heaven. Please know that you will always remain together, for your love for each other is an impenetrable bond which can never be broken. You nurtured your love throughout the length of your lives. Your reward is sharing your presence with each other forever."

I watch both of them as they move closer and closer to the bridge. There is such a sense of peace and joy surrounding them. When they reach the bridge, they both turn around and take one last look at the meadow where they met. They are both so grateful to be together once again. They turn back and walk across the Rainbow Bridge, lit up with multicolor feathers to welcome them. These are the feathers of a multitude of angels, animal or otherwise. I am amazed at how their love is made perfect in this very moment as they enter eternal life. I know that one day my loved one will greet me here too, and I'll finally experience this tremendous joy on my own. This will be worth the wait.

Chapter Twelve

COMING TOGETHER

I am allowed to observe a second animal-human encounter on earth.

The hunter came to an open field and pulled out his binoculars to see what animals were in the grassy knoll. There was a small pond nearby, which he thought would attract larger animals, whether it was deer or fowl. His trip so far had been without success, and he was hoping to have some meat for the winter months to sustain his family living off the grid. He kept watching patiently and pulled out his thermos to drink some coffee. Then he watched as a deer approached the pond.

He got his rifle ready and looked through his sights. He took final aim and pulled the trigger. The deer dropped quickly and moved slightly for a few more minutes. He got up with some of his gear to see if the deer was still alive. If it wasn't dead, he would have to shoot again at close range so it didn't suffer. Just as he approached, something caught the corner of his eye. Two fawns slowly approached their mother and began to nuzzle her. When she didn't move, they laid down next to her and closed their eyes.

It was heartbreaking. He put the deer on his cart so he could bring her to his truck. He didn't want her meat to spoil, but he also didn't want to gut her in front of her fawns. He did care about being humane and only hunting animals for food as needed. He couldn't bring himself to shoot animals just for sport, because they had a right to live just as he did. The fawns followed even as he drove away. He drove slowly enough so they could follow him to his farm. He and his family would have to care for the fawns until they were old enough to fend for themselves. That's the least he felt he could do for them. The hunter thought, "Oh my! I wish I didn't have to feed my family this way. I feel so sorry for her babies."

I see the mother deer at the gate. She is admitted quickly because of the trauma she had experienced. She is in a daze, not quite understanding where she is. She doesn't see her fawns either, and she is very worried about them.

The beagle angel approaches me and directs me to go and comfort the mother deer. He smiles as he gives me wings of my own. I just look at the beagle angel in amazement, because I don't know what is going on.

He says, "God is very pleased with how you've taken an interest in everyone, both their souls and their circumstances. You've been given an additional gift of being able to see both here in the meadow and on earth. What you are now able to see will comfort the souls waiting here because you can explain how their loved ones are faring."

I can't believe that an old toad would be given such a gift. I'm one of the lowliest of the amphibians, who stays close to the ground around water. I don't encounter most humans or animals, so I ask the beagle angel, "Why? I'm not that special."

He replies, "It's because of the beauty and purity of your soul. God asked me to show you what to do in case my loved one appears to walk with me across the Rainbow Bridge. You've done well!"

I walk over to the mother deer as she looks around for any familiar sites. I say, "Do you know where you are?"

She replies, "No. I'm very worried about my babies though. They're too young to survive on their own. Can you give me any information about them or where I am?"

I tell her that I just received my wings, so I'm still learning about the ways in the meadow, but I can get the beagle angel if I can't answer something. I look down through the translucent cloud to where her fawns are, and I see the hunter's wife feeding them formula in a bottle. They are gobbling it up and wagging their tails. Their children were also brushing the fawns and soon it will be time to bring them into the barn.

I look back at the mother deer and say, "I can see them at the hunter's farm, and his family is taking very good care of them." I continue, "Please understand that the hunter was very sorry when he shot you once he saw your two babies. He was trying to provide food for his family over the winter, but he ended up depriving your fawns of your motherly care. He took your body back to the farm so they would follow him. He really understood that they're too young to survive in the wild. Your fawns will be fine."

She breathes a sigh of relief. I tell her that one day she will see her babies again and they will never be separated. The beagle angel joins us and looks upon the mother deer with compassion. He then says, "Would you like to see how your fawns are doing?"

She looks up with intense surprise mixed with longing for her own flesh of her flesh. She blurts out, "YES!!"

The beagle angel says to both of us, "This isn't normally allowed, but God has looked upon your sorrow and has given you the gift to look into life upon earth. He knows that you would not be able to rest and enjoy your time in the meadow with other waiting souls if he didn't comfort you. So please look through that cloud over there near the pond. Once it separates, you will be able to see your babies."

She watches as the hunter's family washes them, feeds them, and plays with them. She smiles with such pride that they are smart enough to survive even if it's with a little help. When she feels convinced they were safe, she says to both of us, "I'm so grateful to you for showing me that they are fine. I was so worried. One of the things about being a creature in the wild is that you never know when danger will appear. It's not so much a concern for myself, but rather my young ones. I just want them to have a chance to grow up. I realize I'm seen as food, but it's not often realized that I have a family of my own too. So, thank you!"

I tell the mother deer that she is welcome to remain in this spot. Other souls will pass by as they also enjoy the serenity and peacefulness of the meadow, so she will have some company too.

She appreciates that she is not alone. She also asks if one of her fawns would be able to wait with her in the meadow until both of her children arrive.

I reply, "Yes, and if you like you can also wait for the hunter to join you. He does feel very guilty about shooting you. If he had seen the fawns, he never would've hunted you."

The mother deer nods yes, as she understands he meant no harm.

I continue to watch the mother deer as she basks in the light. While I understand her pain of suddenly leaving her fawns, I left earth after living a full life. I had plenty of time watching my young ones grow up and giving them the guidance they would need to survive. Life on earth isn't supposed to be easy. However, there is a greater purpose to what happens to each of us. If we never had suffering, then we would never know joy. If we never failed, we would never know success. If we never saw another living being suffer and felt their pain, we would never know compassion. Everything works out for our good in the end, even if we can't see that in the moment.

The mother deer continues to watch her children through the cloud several times a day. She needs to feel close to them and prays that they can feel her love for them. Every once in a while both of them look up to the sky, and she hopes they connected in some way at that moment. The hunter's children take turns brushing her fawns and feeding them. They are still too small to be out on their own, and they still don't know about predators.

The beagle angel comes over to the mother deer one day and he sits with her watching. She looks over and her soul just beams.

He had asked some of the other waiting animals to surround the mother deer so she will not feel so alone. Everyone is waiting for their loved ones, so each soul knows what she is experiencing. Each points out some things they see as she is watching her children. One shows her the fenced-in area where her fawns can run and explore. Another shows her the pets the family has and how they help to teach them some things about nature. A third points out that her children are growing in size and beginning to find foliage for themselves so they can eat rather than being fed.

I come over to the mother deer and speak, "Even though the separation is difficult, while you are waiting here you can watch your children any time you want to see how they're doing. So, you can see every adventure they set off on and actually be with them throughout their entire lives, which you couldn't have done while on earth. Once they grow up and have children of their own, you will be able to watch them also. While it feels like the separation is long, once they join you time stands still as you cross the Rainbow Bridge never to be separated again. You'll understand at the appointed time."

The mother deer puts her head down and asks, "How long have you been here? You seem to have much understanding of what happens and what souls experience."

I reply, "I actually don't know how long, because time is different from what we knew it to be on earth. It's been a while, but I've learned so much about what others experience here. It's quite amazing how different we are, yet we are all alike."

The mother deer nods her head in acknowledgement.

Animal souls speak different languages just like the many languages human souls speak, but everyone understands each other clearly here in the meadow. It's more thoughts than actual words, which is amazing. The longer I am here, the more I efficiently I can read thoughts.

I know the mother deer was young when she was killed, which will make her wait even longer unless her children meet the same fate. However, she gets to rest now in a safe place and that's comforting for her.

The beagle angel joins us once again. He says to the mother deer, "One of your children is on his way to join you. Unfortunately, he was hit by a car and didn't survive. We won't allow you to watch the accident, which is why the opening in the cloud closed for you."

The mother deer stands up and asks where she should wait. The beagle angel nods toward heaven's gate. She looks in that direction and sees her child. She moves toward one of her now-grown fawns and calls out. The child looks at his mother with sheer delight, reflecting the unbreakable bond between mother and child. They catch up with each other and run through the meadow in search of a cool spot to rest and share their experiences while they were apart. Then they will both head to the cloud to watch their other family member. Life goes on.

They both continue to watch the other grown fawn. She is able to have children of her own, and she is a very protective mother. They begin to reminisce about when they were all together.

Finally, the mother asks about the hunter and his family. Her son lowers his head and says with a deep sigh, "He was so very upset that he shot you. He cried as he drove us to his farm, which led his wife and kids to quickly remove us away from the truck. They brought us to the barn and gave us some food and water. They really did care about us and kept us with them until we were old enough to be on our own."

The mother deer asks if they saw her after that, and her son says, "No, they just kept us distracted as you were prepared for their food for the winter months. We never saw what happened to you, and I'm glad that we didn't. It's very difficult to lose your mother but it would've been even more so if we watched you being cut up for food. We were able to grow up in a loving environment and roam within the holding area. When we were ready to be on our own, the gates were opened and we could leave whenever we were ready. We stayed together though, and never strayed too far away from each other."

I watch mother and son together once again. It is nice to see that they were never far from each other's thoughts. Even though tragedy is very painful, it kept them close as they approached eternal life. Suffering does have a purpose when it happens, because living on earth in a physical form or body isn't living in a perfect world. It's a world that not only teaches us about our imperfections, but with the help of others we can overcome them and mature. Suffering can bring about hate or it can generate forgiveness, depending upon what path we choose.

They both continue to look at the remaining adult child through her lifespan. She is one of the lucky animals in the wild to live a full life. It gives both of them joy to watch her family grow and fend for themselves. It is a sign of a job well done, with a little luck thrown in.

The beagle angel walks by and rests near us. He smiles as he tells the mother deer that her daughter is arriving at the heavenly gate very soon. He says, "She lived to a ripe old age and was well loved by her children and grandchildren. Also, the hunter has passed away and he will be arriving shortly also. It will give all of you a chance to see that everything always turns out for the best, even if we can't see it at the moment. No one needs to worry when they trust in God's goodness."

Just like on cue, the mother deer's daughter approaches the gate and walks into the meadow. Mother and son start moving toward her. The daughter deer looks up and is frozen with delight, but she doesn't yet approach them. She is waiting as the hunter also walks through the gate. The daughter deer nods to the hunter and then turns her head toward her family. The hunter's eyes open wide as they follow the beagle angel further into the meadow. Everyone just stands there taking in the moment of being together once again, knowing that everyone is okay. Relief sets in.

The hunter is the first one to speak. He looks at the mother deer and says, "I am so sorry for shooting you and leaving your two fawns as orphans. Taking care of them until they were ready to be on their own was the least I could've done for you. I'm so glad to see you alive and well once again. You look so happy!"

The mother deer thinks for a moment and replies, "I watched how you and your family loved my children. I am very grateful. Things happen because we can't see everything clearly when we are in our earthly bodies, but you did the right thing to make up for it. I forgave you a long time ago. I know how guilty you felt over what happened, but I saw your compassion grow for living things."

The beagle angel speaks to all of the them, "I need to ask the hunter if you would like to wait for your family to join you, or would you like to walk across the Rainbow Bridge with the deer family?"

The hunter says, "I am so grateful that this deer family has remained intact despite my mistake in killing the mother. I'm experiencing such relief from my guilt that I really would like to walk across the Rainbow Bridge with this deer family that I've come to love as my own. My family members will find me in eternal life when their time comes. I'm not worried."

I watch as the beagle angel nods toward the bridge and says, "It's time for you to cross."

The deer family surrounds the hunter and they slowly approach the Rainbow Bridge. Once there, they turn to wave goodbye and walk across as a misty veil surrounds them.

I can no longer see them. The beagle angel notices my solemnness and speaks, "There's no reason to feel sadness because there are no goodbyes in eternal life. You just haven't walked across the Rainbow Bridge yet because you are waiting for the woman. We are all one in eternity and since there is no time, we 'are' just as God is 'I am.' You will see them again."

I look forward to that day, even though I don't understand it. The beagle angel adds, "Since God allowed you to become an angel —albeit in training for a while—you can go back and forth across the Rainbow Bridge just as I do. That's why I'm able to explain so many things to you. It is a great honor to be chosen by God for a higher purpose, so give thanks to Him for the gifts He has given you."

I nod to the beagle angel in silence, because I still need to take all of this in. I don't know why I was chosen or how I became worthy of being chosen.

Chapter Thirteen

PREPARATIONS

I watch a little two-year old boy laying in his crib watching his calico fantail goldfish. He is very still as he moves his head closer toward the glass bowl. The fish also watches him with interest as his tail and side fins move back and forth. The little boy likes the orange, black, and gray colors which glow when sunlight shines through the glass. There is even a touch of blue around the fins. It mesmerizes the boy and calms him when he is home from his cancer treatments.

The goldfish was accustomed to the family leaving her for periods of time for the boy's treatments, but they had arranged for someone to take care of the fantail daily. The little boy had an aggressive brain tumor removed shortly after his first birthday. Then he had a series of both radiation and chemotherapy to try to prevent its return or spread to other parts of his body. He experienced some developmental delays because of the seriousness of his illness, but he loved to just watch his goldfish.

People tend to think that goldfish and other small creatures don't have much room for a thinking brain, but that's not correct. Perhaps what they experience isn't processed in quite the same way as humans, but every living creature thinks in a way that guarantees survival, and they feel pain and emotion as well. I know because I am an old toad who has learned quite a bit, and I feel even more about what I experience. I just couldn't relay that to different creatures when I was on earth because we don't speak the same language. Nonetheless, we are living beings with souls.

This one day as the boy and the goldfish were staring at each other, the boy began to have a seizure. His mother was close by, so she heard him hitting the crib's side rails. She immediately called for an ambulance and then tried to protect him from hurting himself as he thrashed about. The paramedics arrived very quickly and stabilized the boy, all the while obtaining his medical history. They asked the mother to call the neurosurgeon to have him meet them at the hospital.

As one of the paramedics picked up the little boy, he began to have another seizure. The boy was almost dropped as he began to slip out of the paramedic's arms. The other paramedic came around to help support the little boy, ensuring his safety, but no one noticed that the glass fishbowl had gotten knocked over in the excitement. The boy was placed on the stretcher and the ambulance sped off once the boy was reevaluated. His mother followed behind the ambulance to the hospital.

I am talking with the beagle angel as both of our sets of wings move us slowly toward the gate of heaven. The fantail goldfish is with the lion and the lamb. The beagle angel says to me, "It will be a few minutes before the fantail will be allowed in. Let's move further into the meadow to see what is happening at the hospital. Once we know the little boy's condition, we will be able to meet the fantail at the gate."

So we look through the heavenly clouds down to earth. The boy had stopped seizing but the neurosurgeon was very concerned. He ordered an MRI of the brain to see if there were any other changes since surgery. The boy's mother called her husband to ask him to leave work and join her, because she was certain decisions would need to be made about what to do next. The little boy was stable for now, though, as the medication he was given started taking effect. We can go back to the gate of heaven now and greet the goldfish.

The goldfish waits patiently at the gate. He is busy observing what others are doing inside heaven's gate. Finally, his attention turns to the beagle angel and me. The beagle angel asks the lion to open the gate. He nods toward the goldfish as he pushes it open. When the goldfish comes through, he immediately focuses on the pond across the meadow. He moves toward it as we follow him. Conversation will come once he adjusts to his new environment. We watch as he enters the water but remains at the surface. Then he turns to face us.

The beagle angel asks him if he has any questions. The goldfish asks, "Where am I?"

The beagle angel turns toward me and says, "Why don't you take this from here? I need to go back to heaven's gate."

So I look at the goldfish and ask, "What do you remember?"

He replies, "Not much. I was watching my little boy and then he started moving strangely and gasping for air. I was very afraid for him and I couldn't call out for help. Luckily his mother heard the noise he was making as he thrashed about in the crib. The ambulance came quickly but the crew didn't see my glass bowl in the midst of their activity. It was knocked over and I felt life slowly slipping away as they worked on my little boy. The last thing I saw was them quickly taking him downstairs to get him to the hospital. I wish I knew how he's doing."

I tell him that we can watch at some point if he likes, but it's best that he acclimates to his new environment. I tell him that he is fine now, but that he has left his earthly body. I further explain, "When souls arrive and pass through heaven's gate, they need to rest in the meadow for a while. While they are okay, there is energy used in passing through the tunnel after shedding their bodies. It takes time for the soul to re-form once it's not restricted by whatever body the soul has been assigned by God. Each soul then develops more clarity about everything once it's free."

The goldfish nods in acceptance of what he doesn't yet understand. He asks, "How long have all these other souls been here?"

I reply, "It depends on several things. One thing is how long it will take their loved one to arrive. Only God knows the answer to that question, but there is no time continuum here. So the wait never feels long. Every soul just mingles with the other souls around him or her. Another thing to note is that souls at this point still have their gender, which was needed to populate the earth as God saw fit so His Creation continues. Gender will disappear over time as the soul embodies its true form in union with God."

The goldfish opens his eyes wide upon hearing this as if to say "WOW!"

I continue, "The second thing is how many loved ones each soul needs to wait for. Sometimes there are two or three dearly beloved souls bound so strongly in love that those bonds can never be broken even in eternal life. Finally, God will call those forward and ask them to cross the Rainbow Bridge. When souls reach this point, God has prepared a place for them where they will remain forever both with their loved ones and Him."

The goldfish starts to move about the pond while remaining at the surface. He needs to take in all of what I've said. His own movement provides a level of calm for him to process this new information. I just let him be, knowing that he will reach out when he's ready. I'm very happy that he isn't afraid. I will show him how his little boy is doing when he asks me to.

One of the things I've learned from the beagle angel is that there's no rush to get souls through the process of entering eternal life. Everything happens seamlessly when it's supposed to happen. No one can control the flow of a river. Sometimes the water moves quickly, other times very slow. Eternal life is fluid, not stagnant, and everything is determined by God.

The beagle angel moves closer to the pond as he also observes the goldfish. He turns to me and says, "Even angels don't know what God thinks or what His plans are for each and every soul. We listen to get some instruction as to how God wants to proceed, but sometimes we don't hear anything, so we just wait. This is one of those times. God knows what is happening with the little boy, as well as when he will arrive here. That's not for us to know. Our purpose is just to support the souls who rest here until they rejoin their loved ones."

I nod in understanding. I tell him that I am grateful for all that I've been shown.

He smiles and adds, "You were very interested in what was happening both here and on earth. You truly care about others and want to help. God is impressed by how unselfish you are. You aren't so full of only your own self-interests that God doesn't have room to enter. You empty yourself when you refocus your attention on the concerns of others. When you empty yourself, God is able to fill you with the gift of Himself. When this happens more and more, you are on your way to not only being an angel but also a saint."

I take in all of what the beagle angel says. It seems to me that life on Earth is where souls develop as each goes through a range of experiences. It's not always easy, and when we're in the middle of situations we don't understand, we sometimes flounder. If previous experiences don't allow us to work our way through a range of emotions, the unknown creates uncertainty. Yet God knows what we are going through and what we need, if we only find a way to ask Him for help. This is what I learned when on earth even though I was just a toad. I was the head of my toad family though, so I observed everyone and everything to help my family survive. Life can be so interesting if we take the time to watch and listen to what's not being said.

The beagle angel motions toward the goldfish as he says, "It's time to show him what his young child is going through." He moves toward the goldfish and points toward the clouds, which open up to the young boy on earth. The goldfish watches as the doctors rush him into surgery to try to correct what the MRI showed. The tumor had returned and was growing into blood vessels in the boy's brain. There was some bleeding that needed to be stopped. The young boy's parents are crying as they pray for their child to come through this. The goldfish also is devastated.

The beagle angel asks both of us to move toward Heaven's Gate. We see the lion sitting up and looking toward the tunnel by which souls travel. The lamb moves gently toward the tunnel opening and holds the soul of the young boy as soon as he appears. The lamb brings the young soul to the gate and releases him ever so gently so he can approach us. The fantail goldfish is so ecstatic as his sorrow disappears. The young boy reaches out to his beloved fantail, and all of his loneliness from leaving his family disappears. He knows he is safe and surrounded by love.

The beagle angel motions for both of them to proceed further into the meadow. They both need time to embrace each other and to realize that all is not lost. Love is never lost because that bond is infinite and eternal.

The beagle angel turns to me as we watch from a distance and says, "They need time to acclimate both to each other and being outside of their physical bodies, those vessels that contained their souls. The soul still retains some semblance of form once it exits from the tunnel or conduit transporting it. It will gradually dissipate just as fog does to be more freely moving like a cloud. The brain and spinal cord are the connection with our divine Creator, and they begin to merge with God's formless essence once they fully enter eternal life."

I follow the beagle angel as he moves closer to the Rainbow Bridge. He asks me to tell the young boy and the goldfish that God would like them to move across the Rainbow Bridge. The place He has prepared for them is ready and he has lined it with the tapestry of their love.

I approach both and repeat what I was told. I watch as they look at each other and draw close to each other as they move toward the Bridge. Their happiness permeates the area and leaves a discernible trail of joy. Once they are at the Rainbow Bridge, God's own love for them pulls them gently toward Him and into eternity. Their journeys are complete and now everlasting. Their purpose has been fulfilled.

Chapter Fourteen

SILK THREADS

I am surprised to see a duck walk through Heaven's Gate unannounced. She is just as surprised to be here. Her exit from earth happened so suddenly. I meet her as she looks around to see where she might be. I find out that she was one of five ducklings that had been cared for by her farmer and the farmer's wife. They also took care of her parents and always made sure they were safe from predators traveling through their property. The duck's family of seven were quite comfortable and were often joined by other duck families who visited the farmer's large pond. Life was good.

I watched duck families when I was on earth, as we often shared the same wetlands and waterways. Male and female ducks are mates for life, taking care of each other as they grow older. It is devastating for one of the spouses to die, and the survivor goes through a long period of mourning for their lost mate. Both mother and father watch over their ducklings carefully, and they encircle them when swimming to make sure they all stay together. So, I'm surprised when this one duckling approaching adulthood arrives at the meadow. She looks lost as I approach her.

I introduce myself to the duck as she smiles. I say, "It looks like you came here very suddenly. I'm wondering what happened, if you don't mind talking about it?"

The duck replies, "Well, I don't rightly know myself. The last thing I remember is the farmer and his wife scurrying around as the skies darkened and the winds picked up. They were quite a ways away from the farmhouse as they were trying to retrieve my family and me from the pond. They could only carry one of us under each arm and the farmer's wife had a couple of extra pockets in her apron. There wasn't room for me—I was the biggest duckling—so I tried to follow behind them as they made their way to the storm cellar."

The duck continues, "Everyone was about fifty feet from the cellar when the winds picked up. I was too light to walk into the wind, and the air was too turbulent to fly. I saw everyone get to the cellar. The farmer got everyone inside and then turned to come back for me. However, the skies had darkened and this huge funnel cloud was approaching. The farmer almost didn't make it back to the storm cellar, but as he grabbed a hold of the door, he saw the funnel scoop me up and toss me around as he shut the door. That's the last thing I remember. I miss my family and I don't know where I am. Is my family here somewhere?"

I just look at her, thinking about how traumatic her experience was. I've weathered some storms in my lifetime on earth, but nothing like this. I don't know what to say as her eyes plead for some kind of explanation and information about her family. I look for the beagle angel because I need some advice on how to handle this, but he is nowhere to be found. I learn later that God had asked him to go to earth in order to protect the farmer, the farmer's wife, and the rest of the duck family during the storm. No one knew why this particular duckling was brought to Heaven's Gate now. God doesn't always share what His reasoning is.

I explain to the duck that she is in a waiting place until her loved ones can arrive, and that she can enjoy the meadow and pond as well as meet other souls waiting. I point to the Rainbow Bridge in the distance and tell her that is the entrance into eternal life. Once her loved ones arrive and they are reunited, they will walk across the bridge together, never to be separated again.

Her eyes light up with amazement. "I can't wait!" she says. She begins to explore while I keep watch over her reactions to everything. I too want her to feel safe.

I watch her effortlessly mingle with other souls. The duck has a very gentle, trusting nature. She wants everyone to feel welcome and appreciated for who they are. I can't second guess God, but perhaps He wants this loving soul in heaven for some reason? I can guess at this, but I'll never know for sure what God thinks. I know the number seven symbolizes the "perfect" or "completion," and this duck was the seventh in line on the way to safety. Again, I can only surmise that her job was done. I'm not all-knowing, nor is any soul. We tend to forget that when we think we are in control of our own lives. We don't create our own destiny; destiny finds us, and often when we least expect it.

I'm so lost in my own thoughts that I don't see the beagle angel sitting quietly next to me. I'm startled as I refocus.

The beagle angel tells me, "I'm back from the dangerous tornado that tore through the duck family's rural town. They're safe, as is the farmer and his wife. Many others aren't so lucky. I know we have the one duckling God wanted to return home."

I ask, "Why did God need her to return?"

The beagle angel smiles and replies, "I don't know. No one knows when and why their lives end on earth. No one is privy to God's thoughts and intentions except to catch a phrase here or there as we pray. No one is really in control, although we like to think that we are. We just have to wait and see what happens. At some point many things will become clear."

I turn to watch the duck again who's adjusted very well to her new place. I ask the beagle angel what it was like after the tornado disappeared. He said that there's devastation everywhere, but a few lives were lost and there were many injuries. He added that it will take much time to rebuild, since money has become more important on earth in recent years than helping one's neighbor. Greed has led to the accumulation of vast amounts of wealth in the hands of a few, and those individuals don't want to share it. The realization is lost that there's only a certain amount of money to go around for everyone, so many go without. However, most of all, God is the One who provides everything including money. If we let go of what God has given us and use it for the common good, we make room for God to give us more.

I ask the beagle angel, "Do you think we can show the duck that her family is okay?"

He says, "Let's give the duck some more time to be with other souls. Her family, the farmer, and the farmer's wife also need time to recover from and sift through the damage to their property. It's best the duck see them once they've come out of the shock of devastation."

I sigh, knowing how nature can be a brutal force at times. Thinking out loud I say, "Yes, it's best to wait a little while. There's no rush to see how things have happened when we trust in God to take care of every aspect of our lives." Then I go deep into my own thoughts of what I think eternal life would be like.

The young duck is enjoying her time in the meadow. She loves the natural, peaceful scenery. She is happy that the souls around her accept her without question. When she thinks about the storm that separated her from her family, she just swims around peacefully to regain her strength. She remembers being in the funnel cloud and being thrown against other objects in the funnel. The last thing she remembers is being thrown from the funnel against the wall of a building that had collapsed. Then she arrived here.

I ask the duck if she felt any pain.

She says, "No, everything happened so quickly and I died upon impact. I tried my best to see my family while I was being thrown about, but I knew that I was quite far away from where the funnel cloud picked me up. I miss them! Once I left my body, I didn't feel anything except that I was floating in this dark tunnel. Then I saw a white light at the end of the tunnel, which seemed to pull me through and set me in front of Heaven's Gate. I'm comfortable now, except for the feeling of pain of being separated from my loved ones."

I nod in understanding and motion for her to continue her swim. The beagle angel is watching nearby and gently moving his wings back and forth. He is generating peace through his movements. He watches the young duck and feels compassion for her. Life has a way of changing circumstances very quickly and when you least expect it.

He then looks at me and says, "You miss your family too and the woman who cared about you, don't you?"

I look at him with tears in my eyes and reply, "Yes, very much so."

The beagle angel continues, "Do you truly understand that this time of separation is short and that God will bring you back together again?"

I nod, but add, "Yes, I do, but I don't yet know what eternal life will bring. I guess that's where faith and trust come in." The beagle angel smiles in agreement.

I ask the beagle angel if it now might be time to allow the young duck to look through the cloud to see her family. He tells me to use my experience gained so far, and to also empathize with all the duck had gone through and was now feeling. I think she is strong enough now, and that it is time to bring her to a greater understanding of what is to come. I turn to the beagle angel for approval but he has moved away. I smile and know that it is my time to start making decisions. So I approach the duck.

She stops swimming around when she sees me. She swims toward the edge of the pond as I stand by the water.

I ask her, "Would you like to see how your family is doing after the storm?"

She perks up and says with surprise, "Yes! How do I do that?"

I motion for her to follow me and point toward the cloud we will be approaching. Once we get there, I explain that I want her to keep looking at the cloud. The cloud starts moving and gradually becomes less nebulous until there is an opening. The duck's eyes open wide and she begins flapping her wings with enthusiasm as she looks down toward where her home was on earth. She cries when she sees her family and the devastation the tornado had left from passing through.

The duck turns toward me and asks, "Is my family alright? I don't see the house and the barn. The truck is on its side and all of the crops are strewn about."

I speak as gently as I can, "They have been through so much, but most of all they are very worried about you. They couldn't find you. Your duck parents are fine and so are your four siblings. The farmer and his wife got them into the storm cellar in time, but they did see you taken up by the tornado."

The duck asks if there is any way to let them know that she is okay.

I say "No, but if they pray for you, perhaps God will bring them the peace of knowing you're fine."

The duck keeps watching to see if she can see them somewhere on the landscape. I tell her that the farmer and his wife are helping neighbors, so just keep watching for a while longer. We gaze in the direction of the pond on the farm, and the duck is able to see her duck family. They stick very close together out of fear of being separated, just in case another storm comes through. As we look beyond the pond to the road, we see the farmer slowly walking back to where the house stood.

I see the beagle angel coming toward us, and he starts watching the farmer. He tells both of us that the farmer's wife has passed away, after the ceiling collapsed while she was in a neighbor's house helping to gather some of their things.

The duck lets out a cry and asks, "What will happen to her? The farmer will be so lonely."

The beagle angel speaks gently, "She will be joining you here very shortly. You are free to decide if you would like to walk with her across the Rainbow Bridge or if both of you would like to wait for the farmer and the rest of your duck family."

The young duck thinks this over but still has many questions. She asks, "If we do across the bridge, will I ever see my family and the farmer again?"

The beagle angel says, "Yes, you will because love is never lost. Those we love are always near to us, and love always has a way of finding its way home."

The duck looks at me and asks, "What do you think I should do, old toad? You've been here for a while, and you are still waiting. What is to be gained if the farmer's wife and I go across the Rainbow Bridge? Will she want to?"

I answer, "I think that's a personal choice. You have someone you love who is able to walk across with you. Once you enter eternity the options are limitless. You will both be with God and He only unites. He never divides the threads of love. I've not entered eternal life, so I can't fully give you an answer."

The beagle angel pipes in, "I've gone back and forth across the bridge many times to help those arriving in the meadow find loved ones who decided to walk across with the first loved one who arrived. If you are on the other side, once additional loved ones pass through Heaven's Gate, you will be directed to move toward the Rainbow Bridge on the eternity side to meet your loved ones as they walk across to join you. You will always find them."

The young duck says that she wants to walk across the bridge with the farmer's wife. Just at that moment the farmer's wife hears the duck's wishes as she approaches. Both are so happy to see each other that neither wants to disappoint the other. They both look back and forth between the beagle angel and me. We both motion in unison to approach the Rainbow Bridge. The duck and the farmer's wife look at each other, and in happiness approach the bridge. As they start to walk across, they feel almost like they are being guided across by some power that surrounds them with the love that passes all understanding. They turn to wave to us and then disappear in the Rainbow mist. God awaits.

Chapter Fifteen

THE CROSSING

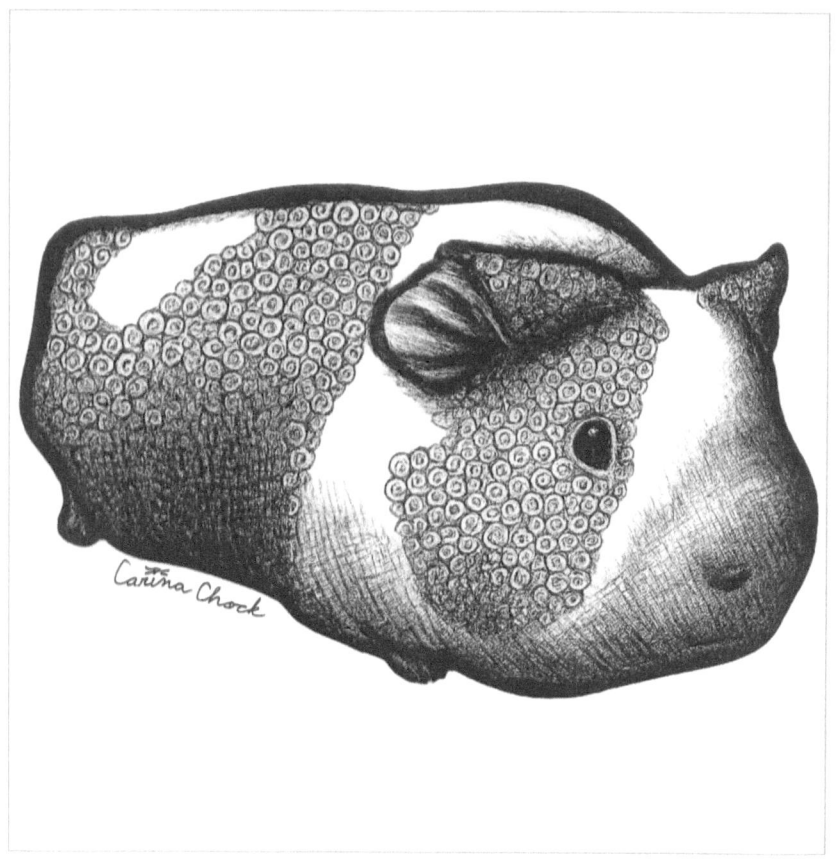

I watch this scene with the beagle angel. It is one of many life situations we observe in order to keep tabs on what is needed after a soul passes through Heaven's Gate. We see a guinea pig surrendered to an animal shelter once his family was evicted. They brought all of his toys, his cage, the remaining food, and his papers. It was a sad moment for the family of four, but the shelter wouldn't allow them to keep any pets. The person at the animal shelter asked the family if they would like a foster to watch their guinea pig, just in case their circumstances changed soon.

They asked how long the person who fostered could keep the guinea pig for them, but they knew they couldn't pay for his needs during this time. The person said that there was funding to help people short term in cases just like this, with the hopes of reuniting families with their pets once again; the family was told there was no commitment on their part except to keep the shelter informed of their situation. This gave them hope and one less worry as the parents tried to find work after being laid off. Their five- and seven-year-old children were relieved to think they would see their pet once again soon.

The family was sad, but they were able to understand. However, the guinea pig could not and was traumatized. One of his toys was an exercise wheel, and he kept riding it for hours.

Everything depended upon the parents finding work and a place to stay. It's very difficult when jobs are suddenly lost—far too many families live paycheck to paycheck just to buy the most basic necessities. This family asked to stay with relatives or friends until their situation improved, but it wasn't possible. Everyone was hoping this was just temporary. The family visited their pet once a week, but it wasn't the same. They even thought about sneaking the guinea pig into the homeless shelter, but they were afraid of being thrown out.

Time went on. Days turned into weeks, and then it became several months with no change in their situation. The family was getting very discouraged. One of the most painful things for anyone is having to leave a pet because they can't afford to keep it. This especially affected their seven-year-old who was the one begging her parents for the guinea pig. She loved her guinea pig very much, and she cried every time she went back to hold him. The guinea pig just kept licking her tears away and became very anxious once the family left.

I turn to the beagle angel and almost cry myself as I say, "How can this happen? Why can't even the homeless find acceptance of their pets in temporary housing? Most loving pet owners take very good care of their pets and will gladly pay if there is accidental damage. I just don't get it, but perhaps that's because I lived in the wild."

The beagle angel doesn't say anything in reply, but rather starts to move toward Heaven's Gate. I follow. When we get to the gate, he points toward the lamb. I look closely but I can't see anything. The beagle angel bows his head in silence, so I walk outside the gate to get a closer look.

I walk around the lamb and see why the beagle angel brought me here, and I cry out in devastation. Curled up against the lamb's belly is the little guinea pig. He is being comforted by the lamb as he seeks to find the love he lost. I look at the beagle angel, my eyes showing the sadness I now feel. Then the beagle angel gently picks up the guinea pig and bring him through Heaven's Gate. We bring him further into the meadow and continue to keep him close to us, because he is still very young. I ask the beagle angel what happened.

He replies, "This little guinea pig loved his family very much, and he died of a broken heart. Once the seven-year-old girl found out that he died, she also became ill. The girl loved her little pet just as much in return. She's a very sensitive little girl and she could not handle losing her guinea pig in addition to her family losing their home and almost all of their possessions when they were evicted. No one could comfort her."

I go over to the cloud to see if I can view the family's current situation. The seven-year-old was at the hospital, with her parents looking dejected and very frightened. Their five-year-old daughter sat between them crying silently. The doctor came in the room and told them that their daughter had an undetected birth defect affecting her heart. He continued that he would like to operate on her when she was stronger. Her vital signs were weak, and they didn't know when she would wake up from the coma she had entered. The parents prayed for both of their daughters and their living situation. Sometimes life seemed impossibly unfair.

I turn toward the beagle angel as he continues to hold the guinea pig. The little pig is able to watch his family and perk up just knowing they are there. I ask the beagle angel about the seven-year-old, but he just says that we have to watch and wait. He sets the guinea pig down into a tuft of grass so he can continue to be with them from a distance, and we walk to another area of the meadow where we are beyond hearing distance.

Then the beagle angel speaks, "The seven-year-old girl will not survive. She will not wake up from her coma, and God is preparing to receive her home very soon. She also is dying of a broken heart. The strain of losing her beloved pet put such a strain on the birth defect no one knew she had."

I close my eyes to shut out the reality of the moment. I know life on earth can be cruel when things happen without rhyme or reason, but I want to just scream out that this didn't need to happen. The father didn't have to lose his job. Someone could've helped him find something else before he was let go, or perhaps his employer could've made budget cuts in other ways. After he's left his job, no one sees what has happened to his family as a result of losing the income he needed to support his family. No one from work saw that he lost his home, his possessions, his pet, and now one of his daughters. All of this just because money couldn't be found from somewhere to keep him employed.

It's not just the immediate suffering that goes unnoticed. The father will now not be able to afford the care his daughter is receiving without his health insurance benefit. Those who could be responsible for supporting him through this moment won't even realize how their desire to cut costs has affected someone. Even though I lived in the wild, we still observed what was happening and watched out for others around us. Money wasn't important to us as animals, but we saw that it was very important for some people who measured success by how much they could accumulate. The only problem is that this can become greed when large amounts of money are gathered just to hold onto. This prevents it from recirculating in purchases bought and work performed to create and maintain jobs. If money isn't spent, jobs disappear.

Money is finite, so if a few hold onto far more money than they need to live comfortably, there's less for others to live on and buy what they need for their families. This creates a cycle of poverty, which never seems to go away. Sometimes there is a benefit to suffering when it teaches compassion and empathy for others, because we know firsthand what souls are going through when we walk in their shoes. I'm sure it sounds funny to hear an old toad thinking about societal problems, but I have observed much in my lifetime. My soul is capable of experiencing what all other souls experience, no matter which physical body God placed me in while on earth.

I go back to stay with the little guinea pig. I want to be there for him if he needs me. He keeps looking through the cloud at the hospital bed. The little girl still hasn't woken up. Simple hearts which love deeply and innocently are easily broken. The guinea pig cries intermittently. He's not interested in enjoying the surroundings and the other souls in the meadow. He only wants his little girl to wake up even if she can't see him. The doctor and his team walk into the room. They tell the parents that they need to take her to the operating room now even if she isn't as stable as they would like her to be. The parents nod in agreement and sign the consent papers. Then we all pray.

The guinea pig looks at me and says, "There is a lot going on here in the meadow that those on earth aren't aware of happening. It's all behind the scenes, so to speak. It's almost another dimension of life."

I agree, adding, "Yes, when souls are in their given bodies, they are usually prevented from seeing outside of what is happening on earth. Their bodies even prevent them from fully seeing what's happening right in front of them. There are often miscommunications, misinterpretations, and plenty of misunderstandings while people do their best to try to figure out what is going on both inside of themselves as well as those around them. Those who reach out to God in prayer can catch glimpses of Heaven and eternal life, but even then, God only allows certain things to be seen."

The guinea pig turns toward the cloud to see how his little girl is doing. He sees that she is in the operating room with all types of machines making noises. There are many people in the room, each focused on their individual responsibilities. There is also much chaos when her vital signs diminish. The guinea pig continues to watch with sadness. He doesn't see the beagle angel join us, nor does he see the beagle angel shake his head to me—I know then that it will be very soon when she will join us. We convince the guinea pig to move away from the cloud because there is no reason for him to see her die.

We all start toward the meadow where other souls are interacting with each other. We sit down on either side of the guinea pig. The beagle angel speaks gently to the guinea pig, "Please understand that when all living things die on earth, they are not permanently gone. The process of death is the soul leaving the body. The body dies, but the soul continues to live as it returns to its true home, which is with God, Our Creator."

The guinea pig nods his head in understanding. He asks, "Then why does it hurt so much to lose someone?"

The beagle angel answers, "It's because we miss having those we love in our lives. It feels like we'll never see them again, because where their souls have gone is a place we can't see. However, please know that you are in that place now visible, and your loved one will join you very soon. So, let's move toward Heaven's Gate and I will prove this to you. Your little girl is on her way to see you—to be with you—forever."

The seven-year-old girl sees us approaching before the guinea pig has a chance to look up. She runs through the gate and embraces her beloved guinea pig. Love never ends nor does it diminish. Both the little girl and the guinea pig were so young when they died, but now their broken hearts are healed in their reunion. Because they were young, they didn't know that they would recover from their separation; they hadn't yet had the experiences they would need to understand that. The young feel emotions very strongly, especially when they are unpleasant or disruptive. They experience vulnerability before they are emotionally equipped to handle it, so it can leave a lasting physical impact on their wellbeing and health.

The seven-year-old girl's parents and little sister will go through the same grief process. This time, though, the parents will have a better understanding of what the five-year-old girl needs to guide her through this. Life will improve for them, as time heals all wounds. Suffering can make each of us stronger if we approach it with the right attitude, knowing that there is hope in the future if we have faith that things will be better at some point. We begin to learn to take each day as it comes without dwelling on the past and worrying about the future. Today is where "I AM" dwells, and that's where we find God.

The beagle angel says, "Both of you have a decision to make. Do you want to wait for the rest of your family to arrive here in the meadow, or would you like to walk across the Rainbow Bridge into eternal life? There's no right or wrong decision. Either way you will rejoin your family at the appointed time when their earthly journeys are complete."

Both look at each other and say in unison, "I want to walk across the Rainbow Bridge."

We smile and go with them to the edge of the bridge. The rainbow glows with vibrant colors, welcoming them on their new journey toward the other side of the Rainbow Bridge. They walk hand-in-hand, and both know that they are together forever. Love never disappoints, as it is the force that binds us with each other and with God.

Epilogue

I, too, experience my forever when the woman who took care of me dies and joins me. It is a beautiful reunion in the meadow, as the rabbit she loves also joins us, and now we experience how happy each soul is when they saw their loved one approaching them. We walk across the Rainbow Bridge as we wave to the beagle angel. It isn't goodbye—I understood there are never goodbyes in Heaven. The woman, the rabbit, and I move through the mist and stand at the other end of the bridge for a few moments just taking in all of the emotions flooding into our souls. I still have to absorb all that is happening right now because it is so different from life on earth in a physical body. Now my soul is free, as are all of the souls in eternity.

We are each cherished and recognized for who we are in God's eyes, and it's our bonds with those special to us that fulfills our need to be loved. Those who've gone before us never left us.

They've watched over us and prayed for us so we could one day join them forever. Our pets and the other wild living creatures we've taken care of will see us again when we have died, and we will reunite with them. However, this time we will never leave each other. The time of separation will end, and when it does, we won't even remember it in the midst of joy. So we must be patient and learn to trust, knowing that our love for each other is strong. It's worth the wait, because our love continues to grow during this time. The best part of this is knowing that love is really all we have to take with us, and it feeds our souls forever.

Contact Cheryl Price Morgan

If you would like to learn more about Cheryl or her novels, visit her website at https://www.cherylpricemorgan.com/.

FOLLOW CHERYL ON SOCIAL MEDIA

amazon.com/author/cheryl-price-morgan

goodreads.com/cheryl-price-morgan

linkedin.com/in/cherylpricemorgan

About the Author

Cheryl Price Morgan is originally from Niagara Falls, NY. She has been married to her husband, John, for 50 years. While they lived in Milford for many years, they now reside in Oxford, CT with their two dogs. She is a retired respiratory therapist and pulmonary laboratory coordinator where she worked for thirty-five years at St. Vincent's Medical Center in Bridgeport CT. She has a Bachelor of Science degree in Psychology from John Carroll University in University Heights, OH, which is a suburb of Cleveland. She has a Master of Arts in Health Systems Management from Sacred Heart University in Fairfield, CT.

She has been told from the second grade through graduate school that she should write. While writing has always been an interest, her service to her patients and community was a higher priority. Retirement has provided the time to finally write, and she hopes that sharing

her experiences with others might be of value during these unprecedented times. Her first book is "*A Journey Unfolding: The Mystery of Trusting God,*" which you also might enjoy.